MEMOIRS of a SICK MIND
Book 1:

Blood of my Claire

Isaac Hans

MEMOIRS of a SICK MIND
Book 1:

Blood of my Claire

Part I

the first blood

Prologue

Huntsville Texas

"My only regret is that he didn't die."

Crippling despair permeated the stark, concrete walls. The overbearing aura of violence was as normal there as the sun's rise each morning, and the spilled blood of countless men lurked within the smallest cracks and crevices in the floor. Haunting screams of the incarcerated men filled the air – some to be silenced suddenly and never heard again.

Dr. Rand Lorne felt increasingly guilty he'd become desensitized to the constant reminder that there are some places even God's most endearing Angels would never dare enter. He was able to cope by focusing on his job and separating himself emotionally from the inmates he was paid to patch up.

Today's job was nothing out of the ordinary for Dr. Lorne – a high profile, well-known inmate, Ishmael Abias, had arrived at the prison infirmary with a badly slashed hand. The wound was entirely defensive; the doctor saw Ishmael had used his hand to block his face from being slashed – presumably with a homemade prison shank. His assailant, Tyler McBride, was a low-level criminal known for aggravated house and car burglaries at best and had likely been out to make a name for himself.

Ishmael had reported the incident to a senior correctional officer – John Mistry – who had written it all down in bad scrawl in his notebook. Ishmael told the CO he almost died because Tyler had aimed the shank at his neck and face. Fortunately, Ishmael had easily been able to deflect the weapon and force it into his perpetrator's chest. Tyler's ribcage was penetrated deeply but his heart was unscathed. Still, it punctured his lung and nicked an artery, so Tyler was transported to the county hospital. Ishmael simply went to the prison infirmary.

Officer Mistry stood next to the operating table as Dr. Lorne completed the final stiches in Ishmael's hand and wrapped it up in gauze and surgical tape.

"Okay, please try not to use this hand for at least a month," Dr. Lorne told his patient. His voice was flat and emotionless.

"So how the fuck am I supposed to get by in this five-star hotel?" Ishmael snarled.

"Accommodation issues are between you and the Warden. I have nothing to do with…"

"Talk to the Warden, not the Doctor," Officer Mistry interrupted. The frustration in his voice was loud and clear – the man obviously had little patience for his charges. "Come on. Let's go," he snapped.

Ishmael stood up and was led off to a special holding cell. He'd stay there until the Doctor submitted an injury report to the Warden and a decision could be made as to Ishmael's accommodations while his hand healed.

As the cell door closed behind him, Ishmael repeated his initial sentiment.

"I meant what I said," he growled. "I wish the prick had died."

Officer Mistry did not respond.

***

Three weeks later, Officer Mistry arrived at Ishmael's temporary cell.

The day Ishmael was waiting for had finally come; as the CO approached, he stood up and walked backwards to press himself against the cell bars. The bars were cold as ice. After shackling Ishmael's wrists and ankles, Officer Mistry opened the cell door and led Ishmael down the hallway to the meeting room.

Ishmael was ready.

He had planned for this a long time.

It was to be a meeting with a fellow Harvard graduate within the walls where Ishmael could find no equal. He could let his guard down and finally be free.

There was no machismo necessary, no veil of intimidation required, no need to act like the other prisoners he loathed so much. So many of them were in that God-forsaken place for the most heinous crimes against others – many had abused and killed their wives, some had hurt or murdered children, and some had stolen from people with nothing left in the world. A large proportion of the incarcerated had disrupted the social order and caused calamity, resulting in death and destruction, in an effort to push their own political, religious, or moral agendas. Ishmael knew he wasn't like them at all. He *hated* them. He wanted them further punished for their evil, but within the prison walls, he had to act like them just to survive. The shank's gash and subsequent stiches in his hand were mild punishment in comparison to the shame Ishmael felt as he was forced to act like the delinquents around him. Though, he knew that once inside the prison, even those awaiting trial who would be proven innocent, everyone was the same – they all became the scum beneath society's sewers.

It was exhausting, but soon Ishmael would find a temporary reprieve. He entered the meeting room and sat down in the metal chair. Officer Mistry shackled Ishmael's hands and feet to the chair before removing the walking shackles that hung between his prisoner's ankles.

"Remember when I said I wish that bitch was dead?" Ishmael smirked. "I didn't *really* mean it."

As usual, Officer Mistry chose not to respond.

Moments later, Dr. Lance Russell arrived from the door on the opposite side of the room. He approached the seat opposite Ishmael and sat down. He carried no notepad, no laptop, no tape recorder; Ishmael knew he was just here to speak.

"Ishmael Abias…"

Ishmael didn't – couldn't – stand.

"Dr. Russell, you look different than you do on television," Ishmael said. He didn't like the feeling of the restraints holding him to the chair – it reminded him too much of the broken lunchroom desk of his childhood.

The memory was most unpleasant.

Ishmael was a little starstruck to see *the* Dr. Russell in person. On television, the guy looked so polished, but in person, he looked… *imperfect*. He wore a simple a grey suit – its style not modern and well below what the shrink could afford. Ishmael figured he was concerned about keeping his image of being old and well-seasoned in life – a look most befitting for someone so world-renowned, a household name. A modern-looking, sharply dressed psychiatrist might well be misconstrued as one who is too flashy and lacking in life experience. The doc's gray hair wasn't consistent – it was either a bad dye job or he was going silver in a peculiar pattern . His fine lines and wrinkles were visible, his voice seasoned with age. In a way, Ishmael thought that version of him made him much more relatable in person. Maybe not on television, but definitely in person.

"I'm happy you requested to see me, Ishmael. It's good for me too."

"Why is that, Doctor" Ishmael broke his silence. "I have a reason to see you, but surely you are only looking to increase your notoriety. *'Dr. Russell interviews incarcerated Ishmael Abias, Harvard graduate turned killer.'* We've heard it all before."

"Forgive me, Ishmael, but *you* requested to see *me*, and yet you criticize my motivation for agreeing to meet with you?"

Ishmael was taken aback: the psychiatrist had a point.

He also couldn't help but notice how the shrink spoke to him like he was an esteemed Harvard graduate and not some dumb, common psychopath.

And he appreciated that.

"To answer your question, Ishmael, I did not agree to come to bolster my notoriety. You are a household name across the country. However, to me, this is a simple case study. You deserve much more respect than that, but I couldn't do anything about it until you reached out to me."

"Sure."

"I know you have an agenda. You are not some run-of-the-mill criminal. I'm not here to *treat* you, Ishmael – I just want to listen." Dr. Russell leaned back a little in his chair. "So... tell me what led up to this moment. Tell me why you finally decided to confess. Tell me *everything*."

Part I: Chapter One

I was nothing more than a little kid when I first became acquainted with Ashford, Ohio.

That was also the first time I came to realize I was not like the other children I saw around me. Now, there are many who'd be quick to jump to the conclusion that institutional racism is an adult matter and young children should not be subject to discussing such things in order to preserve their innocent, fragile minds.

Frankly, as far as I'm concerned, those who believe such rhetoric tend to be the ones propagating said racism and passing it along to their deeply unpleasant, ugly-ass children.

Only the children benefitting from the institution are given the privilege of maintaining their innocence. The other kids, like my *nigga* self for instance, were forced to grow up too fast in a world that doesn't particularly love them.

So, it all started when my father was transferred to Ashford when I was ten years old. Before that, we'd lived in New York City. Life has no way – or intention - of slowing down in a place like that, and I often found the hustle and bustle of living in NYC to be taxing. But, at such a young age, I had no way of knowing what was good or bad about living where I was, or what it was like living elsewhere.

The big city was the only life I knew.

After the move, as you can imagine, I immediately experienced the full blast of culture shock.

In our first house, my father's company heavily subsidized the mortgage payments, yet my family got to keep all of the equity the property built up. Naturally, I didn't understand any of that back when I was ten, but my parents seemed very happy about it.

Upon moving in, I didn't have much time to get acquainted with my new home town. The school year was due to start in less than a week and my parents insisted I get ahead in my studies. At the time, being a little kid in a brand-new town with countless places to explore, I *hated* them for making me do that. But, over the years, I reached into my heart and found forgiveness – I grew to understand they were fully aware of how unfair life was and felt my education was my ticket out.

However, that's not to say I never got out of the house at all before the new school year began. While my father was busy at his new job, my mother took me and my little sister, Sarah, along on her daily errands. I knew even back then that, if it was up to my father, I'd be locked in my room all day surrounded by textbooks and college-ruled notebooks. My mother wasn't always easy to deal with either, but at least she believed children should be well-rounded in life and not just reclusive bookworms.

I recall vividly, one day in particular, just a few days before school, my mother took me and Sarah to the local bank. As we entered, I noticed a man looking at us; immediately, he glanced toward the security guard before returning his scrutiny back to me, my little sister, and Mom.

Now, I may have been only ten years old at the time, but I knew full-well what that nonverbal communication between the two men meant. I recall the security guard having a gun – he rested his hand on it and closely watched my mother as she signed in to speak to a representative.

And that's when the first guy approached her.

"Excuse me, Miss?" he said. "You don't need to sign in for check cashing. You can go straight to the window. Denise in window three can help you."

"Sir, I have an account and I need to speak to a bank relationship manager," my mom replied politely.

"And what is it concerning?" The guy narrowed his eyes.

My mother looked down at the name tag affixed to his shirt. "Well, Scott, are *you* the bank's relationship manager?"

"No, I'm the greeter," Scott told her, a little put out.

"In that case, I'll state my business to the bank relationship manager."

I couldn't figure out why my mother wouldn't just tell Scott why she was in the bank. Surely, it would have been so much simpler to state her business and move on – he was a bank person, after all.

However, Mom wouldn't do that; it seemed to me as if she had a point to prove by starting shit with the greeter.

It was then that the sorry excuse for a security guard - the one who'd nervously put a hand on his gun when we'd first walked in – approached us.

"Thurra problem yin 'ere?" he asked.

"Sir, am I a threat to you?" Mom squared up to the guy, who was at least twice her size. "Why are you approaching me like this, and why is your hand on your weapon?" She came off to me as being incredibly brave, though reckon the guard and the greeter were likely thinking she was just an awkward *Black bitch*.

"I seen you talking to Scott and I sees aggression," the guard drawled. "An' that's why I got my weapon to hand."

"I'm a customer having customer issues," Mom stood her ground. "All is within the customer and banker relationship. Your services are not needed, but thank you." How she remained so calm, steady, I'll never know.

"Now wait a minute, I just may have to ask you to leave if –"

Scott was interrupted by a pleasant-looking young blonde lady.

"Jerry, it's alright," the lady addressed the guard before turning to my mom. "Ma'am, come with me please. I'm Barbara, and I would love to assist you."

My mother walked with Barbara to a dark wooden desk over in the corner and away from the suspicious eyes of the guard and the greeter; it was nice to be away from them.

"May I please use the restroom?" I asked Barbara.

"Of course, you can, young man." Barbara's smile lit up my heart. "Go ask Officer Jerry to show you where to go."

I did as I was told; Officer Jerry pointed out the customer restrooms, and I headed on my way. The officer sat at a little desk in the corner near the bank's main door; I noticed his keys were laying on the desk.

I went into the restroom, took my piss, and came out. I noticed Jerry's back was turned and nobody paid me any attention at all. Quickly, I returned to the restroom, went into the toilet stall, and waited. The place smelled like rancid fermenting shit and cheap hand soap, but that didn't distract my concentration; the rude guard didn't seem to be very intelligent, nor did the greeter. I was too young to understand what had happened, but my mother was extremely upset by the interaction.

Now, Mom was my worst enemy in the whole world, with her helicopter-parenting style and constant smothering discipline. But, in a way, she was also the best friend I had – especially in our new town. I couldn't bear to see her hurt, and those two men had hurt her – I'd sensed it, even though she'd put on a remarkable show of bravado.

Something had to be done.

Suddenly, I had an idea.

Grabbing as many power towels as I could from the dispenser on the wall, I stuffed the toilet to its brim. Then, satisfied with my work, I flushed.

Just as I'd hoped, the toilet quickly began to fill up.

A few seconds later, the water poured over the brim and splashed onto the tiles.

Truthfully, I had no idea where it was all heading. All I knew was it was the *start* of something and I'd have to make the rest up as I went along. The very best stories are written that way, and it was actually quite invigorating to watch it play out in real life.

I stepped out of the bathroom and cracked open the soda Mom had packed into the backpack that I had slung over my shoulder. The loud, refreshing *hiss* grabbed Officer Jerry's attention.

"Thank you for showing me where to find the bathroom," I told him with a thin smile.

He replied "No problem" without as much as looking at me; he pronounced "no" as "ner." *Ner problem.* Pretty weird.

I stood there for a moment or two, rather awkwardly, and continued slurping loudly at my soda. I made sure to slurp extra loud at the tiny puddles of soda that collect on the lip of the can after every gulp – call it OCD, but it was my thing.

Before long, Officer Jerry stood up and went into the restroom. I was certain my unformed plan would work.

From inside, I heard, *"Dadgumit!"* Jerry ran out of the restroom and approached me.

"*You* did this." He towered over me, his fat belly hanging over his too-tight belt.

"What did I do?".

"The commode. Did you do that?" he shouted at me.

My eyes welled up, twinkling with fresh tears. Luckily, I didn't have to answer the guard's question as Mom came running.

"Excuse me Officer, why are you yelling at my child?" she demanded.

"I could arrest him for this," Officer Jerry growled. "He's damaged bank property in the bathroom!"

"Mommy, I'm so sorry," I sniffled. "I had to go *really* bad and I pooped so much – I'm *so* sorry it smells."

"I am not worried about that," Officer Jerry snapped. "The lavatorial is *overflowing*!"

"I didn't know that," I protested.

"Do you *still* plan on arresting my son, Officer?" Mom stepped toward the big guy, putting herself between him and me.

"God dadgumit!" Officer Jerry yelled again and ran back into the restroom - presumably to try stopping the flow of water I'd created. The greeter hurried across the bank's foyer and went in with him.

Barbara bustled over from her desk to apologize to my mother, but she wasn't interested in apologies.

"Barbara, just let me finish my business and we will be on our way," Mom told her. She then told me to go wait in the car and handed me the car keys. Before I left, I looked over at the officer's desk and glanced at his car keys; he drove a Dodge.

"In the car, Ishmael! Do you hear me?"

"Yes Mom, I got it." I made my way outside.

As I sat alone in our Toyota Tercel, I noticed there were three other cars in the parking lot. There was a beat-up Audi 5000, a Honda Prelude, and an old Dodge of some sort – I didn't recognize the model. The Dodge obviously belonged to Officer Jerry, and we were parked just two spots away...

I don't know what it was about Ashford – perhaps it was something in the air or in the water – but an irrational impulse overtook me. I'd seen my mother disrespected before, back in New York, but those moments had seemed to go along with the situations at the time – I could easily discern the points of view of both sides of the conflict. What happened there in the bank, however, felt much different. I didn't feel like there were two sides to the story; I felt like my mother had lost before she'd even walked in there. It made me furious and, for the first time, I felt my mind step out of reality.

I figured nobody would be watching me because the bank's racist rent-a-cop was busy cleaning up shitty toilet water.

I clambered out of Mom's car and made my way over to the Dodge. As quickly and quietly as I could, I scratched the living Jesus out of the back bumper with Mom's keys. I remember feeling such a rush doing something so incredibly bad. Believe me, I wasn't *that* kind of kid, but the two men in the bank had done *something* to upset my poor mother, and damaging the guard's crappy old car was the least I could do to avenge her.

At the time, it never once crossed my mind that their treatment of Mom could be because she was a black woman in their bleached-white town – but it wouldn't be too long before Ashford taught me such attitudes truly matter to some, or in some cases, entire communities.

For all her faults as a parent, my mother was too well-spoken and classy for those people to treat her like some common criminal. I was just a kid, but I knew I could avenge her at a level I deemed equivalent to theirs. I gave the back of Jerry's Dodge a few more deep scratches before heading off back to our car, where I didn't have to wait long before mom and Sarah came out of the bank.

Once the thrill of what I'd done wore off, I started to get nervous. Surely, I hadn't been seen because nobody came outside to drag me from Mom's Tercel – but I wasn't sure that harsh justice wasn't going rear its ugly head – it had not occurred to me there'd likely be CCTV cameras outside the bank!

Maybe they'd just send a letter home, or have the cop follow us. Or, maybe they saw me vandalize the guard's car but were too busy mopping up toilet water to come out.

I began to get really nervous.

Mom got into the car with Sarah.

"Ishy, don't worry about what happened in there," Mom soothed. "It's okay if you got sick, and I am sorry the officer yelled at... hey, are you okay?" Mom's words, though normal in tone, had a deafening boom; I snapped back to reality.

"I'm fine, Mom."

"No, you're sweating and you look nervous." Mom sounded worried. "Oh, Jesus, is this about that awful officer? You did *nothing* wrong." She slipped the car into reverse and backed out of her parking space.

My eyes were drawn toward Officer Jerry's car, but then, like a guardian angel, a bright yellow Jeep appeared in the parking lot and took up the spot next to the Dodge.

Mercifully, I didn't get much time to look, but for a brief second as Mom drove away, I saw two little kids clamber from the Jeep. All the nervousness left me like a soul leaving a dead body.

Then, when I looked again, the kids were still in the Jeep and the bumper to the Dodge was clean – not a single scratch on it! I'd experienced déjà vu – or was it some kind of vision or hallucination? A shiver ran through me.

"I understand, Mom," I mumbled.

"That's my boy." Mom smiled at me through the rear-view mirror. I figured she thought she'd helped me feel better, and bless her heart for it. The truth, however, was that I'd learned the meaning of vengeance and *that* made me feel good: it was possible to right a wrong by making the aggressor suffer – even though that particular instance had only been inside my head.

I truly wish the incident in the bank had been an isolated incident, the vision I'd experienced, but little did I know then of the life ahead of me in Ashford, Ohio: I had been given a gift. I prayed that night that anything I might do in the future would be rooted in reality and any hallucinations would work solely to bring me comfort and tranquility.

Part I: Chapter Two

Religion played a huge part of the daily lives of Ashford's citizens. I can't recount a single day without someone bringing up their faith to justify an errant thought process or make sense of something that happened:

Oh, you survived a car accident? All praise to God!

Oh, your mama died in a car accident? Well, the Lord taketh away.

Looks like Mr. Crawford was caught cheating on his wife again. No worries, he and his wife slept fine that night because they felt the Lord would forgive him.

Oh wait, but my minority next-door neighbor did the exact same thing. Now prepare to meet the unbridled fury of the almighty Lord!

And that's how the collective morality of Ashford people worked. They relied on God's love for themselves and depended on His wrath to dish out justice unto others.

I spent most of my formative life in Ashford fascinated by the concept, which I later learned is called the Fundamental Attribution Error. Put simply, it pretty much means when *I'm* a fuck up, it's because of a particular circumstance. However, when *you* are the fuck up, that's because that's how you are!

It doesn't just happen on an individual level either: entire religious and racial groups are guilty of the "Error." And that's why, when a woman is raped in one culture, its counteracted with a reminder that rape also happens in opposing cultures. It doesn't negate the heinous act and, all the while, nothing gets done to help the women of the world.

I digress.

Apparently, Ashford folks had always been Religious and used religion to dictate every aspect of their lives – a fact that was never more noticeable than shortly after Reverend Koika died quite suddenly and unexpectedly of a heart attack.

As with most heart attacks in the relatively young—the reverend was only 42—nobody saw it coming, and the entire town fell into mourning. Then, after the prayer service and funeral ceremony were concluded, a replacement minister arrived at the local Church. That was the first time Ashford met Reverend Watts.

Watts' views were different to those of his new flock. They relied upon their own interpretations of scripture and while Reverend Watts was no different in that way, he based his religious ideals more on how he felt Jesus would act in any given situation – WWJD and all that. Reverend Watts valued that above any and all scripture. Therefore, he believed the Church *should* have a place for homosexuals and all other religions should be loved and given respect.

Predictably, Ashford's faithful did not like the new attitude one bit: condemning others was a cornerstone of their existence and manipulating scripture interpretation was a very convenient means by which to do so.

It came as little surprise then that, over time, Church attendance dwindled. Within two years, the place was forced to shut its doors.

By the time my family arrived in Ashford, there was no central hub for the town's collective morality. Some people formed prayer groups in their own homes, but it was never the same as attending institutionalized religion. Reverend Watts quietly disappeared, and nobody knows where he went, although there was a supposed sighting of him in a Target in Minnesota.

The town soon forgot about their liberal minister when they met Jadrich Lima – he moved to Ashford around the same time as us. He wasn't known to be employed, but he still managed to purchase one of the largest homes on Ashford's outskirts. A few months after settling in, Lima purchased the old Church, which had stood empty following Watts' departure.

The first thing Lima did was remove the oversized crucifix on the front of the church; some of the old timer religious fundamentalists took exception, but Lima wasn't too concerned about what anybody thought. Over the following weeks, we saw countless trucks from remodeling firms parked up in front of the building – but nobody ever saw what was going on inside.

I'll get back to Jadrich Lima later.

Before school started, it held an orientation for parents, and both my mom and dad made the decision to attend – which was quite unprecedented.

It was there, for the first time, the other parents saw them together.

A black woman and her white husband…

***

The week after that, I started school.

Because my last name was Abias and Mr. Janicek liked his classroom plans alphabetized, I had the dubious pleasure of a seat in the front row. Almost immediately after we took our places; one of the kids eyed me down when I placed my backpack onto the seat next to him. The kid was noticeably overweight, with a round belly and prominent boy tits; his name tag read: *Brett*. Time to make a new friend, I thought, and I made the first move.

"Hey what's up man? You a fan of Led Zeppelin?" I asked Brett. The question wasn't arbitrary – he wore a Zeppelin shirt; I still hear the riff to *Immigrant Song* every time I think about the band.

"Umm, yeah, sure, I guess," Brett replied; his response didn't seem very genuine to me, but hey, I was the stranger from another city – who was I to judge how people should act?

"So, I moved here from New York City!"

"Cool." Brett's retort was bland. "Hold up a second."

I looked on as Brett left this seat and walked up to the teacher. I couldn't hear everything they were saying, but I definitely heard my new would-be friend mention something about his parents being upset.

A moment or so later, Mr. Janicek stood up and looked around the class. At the back, there were three desks without name tags on them; he strode over to them, moved one of them toward the window – which was pretty far from the other kids – and then walked over to my desk.

"Ishmael, would you mind sitting over there?" Mr. Janicek asked quietly, pointing to the desk he'd just moved.

Now keep in mind, I was only ten years old at the time, so I didn't even think to ask *why*.

Obediently, I did as I was told. I packed up my stuff and went to sit right at the back of the classroom. As I did so, I heard Brett tell a cute girl next to him, "My parents met his parents and they told me to stay away from that *nigger*."

What made it worse was I *knew* Mr. Janicek heard him, and his only admonishment was: "Brett, come on now." It was the fakest display of condemnation I'd ever seen. Not even one day in at my new school and I had never felt so far away from my home in New York City.

Class was mundane. Mr. Janicek introduced himself and went over his classroom rules. He explained how class was to be conducted, how homework was assigned, and so on. Our first activity was to pick a partner and learn as much about each other as we could in one minute. Because it was the first day, Mr. Janicek assigned partners. He paired six kids before he got to me, and then he paused after saying my name out loud. He looked around the class in a way he hadn't done as he'd paired the other kids – his eyes then rested upon a scrawny-looking kid called Mark, and he asked him to be my partner; in retrospect, the way my teacher asked Mark to be my partner was most telling. He put it, "Mark, would you mind being Ishmael's partner… just this once, please?"

Mark agreed.

How could he not?

Once all the students were teamed up, we got to work. Except, Mark and I didn't talk all that much about ourselves: he kept on asking me questions about my family, especially my mom and dad. The kid talked to me like I was some fucking space alien! I guess it was a lack of intelligence on Mark's part that prevented him from being discreet, because unlike like all the other closeted bigots, he just blurted out, "I've never seen someone with a white and a black parent!"

At first, it didn't really bother me; it was the norm for me, after all. To me, it was the same as having different hair color or height. The thought of my parents being in a mixed-race marriage as a negative thing never once occurred to me. I was happy to answer my partner's questions in a peaceful ignorance that kept me warm – right up until he put the cherry on my sundae.

"Aren't they worried about what God thinks?" Mark said with a frown.

"What do you mean – *God*?"

"Well, why would your dad do that?" Mark asked. "My parents told me God would get angry with him for marrying a nigger."

All that time I'd thought Mark was just getting to know me a little better, but it hit me that he saw my lineage as a huge negative. I wasn't angry right away; my first reaction was confusion. I mean, I hadn't questioned him about his crooked teeth or the hundreds of unsightly moles on his neck.

"I don't see a problem with it, Mark," I replied. It was the best response I could come up with.

Seemingly bored by my retort, the kid just shrugged his skinny shoulders and we moved on. Once we'd sat back down at our seats, I heard him tell the pretty girl next to him, "Yeah, so I got paired up with the nigger my parents warned me about."

The girl next to him didn't seem impressed; she rolled her eyes and looked down at her desk.

Defeated, Mark looked around in a desperate attempt to distract from the fact the cute girl next to him hadn't swooned at his feet. Unfortunately for him, a handful of the other kids *had* noticed. I reckoned they agreed with his transparent distaste for me, but such a blasé response from a girl he'd tried to impress weighed far higher in the cringe factor. Mark stared down at his shoes, clearly hoping the condemning looks would go away.

I learned another valuable lesson that day: just how fucking sweet it was to witness an antagonist's embarrassment.

So, that's a fair assessment of my first day as a student in Ashford Ohio. It's not that I was entirely unaware that there were people who didn't like black people – the fact was always at the peripheral of my understanding. But, at the tender age of ten, the concept hadn't had enough time to gel, especially in a cosmopolitan city like New York. I suppose I perceived bigotry and racism as external concepts that happened to everyone else but couldn't possibly happen to me.

Ashford had found its way of beating that sweet naivete out of me within just one day. And, unfortunately, it was only the beginning of many more similar days to come.

***

As far as life at home went – my father worked late and was never really around for much besides paying the bills. I'm convinced he truly believed he had his priorities in order when it came to me and Sarah, but all he seemed to do was come home and yell at me about how school went. It was noticeable to me even then, all he ever asked about was the academic part of my schooling; he didn't bother to ask me if I'd made friends or how I was coping in a school so far away from the only place I'd known as home. Sadly, all my father cared about were the subjects I was taking and when the textbooks were coming in.

***

A week went by.

I was no longer confused by the other students' reaction to me, but I was still unaware of how to work around it. So, I simply took things one day at a time while finding no solace at home, as I knew my academic progress would always be way more important to my parents than my mental health, confidence, and safety.

In the lunch hall, I bought my food and sat myself down at one of the circular tables. The set up was extremely awkward because it was impossible to avoid people, which made it particularly uncomfortable for us introverts.

During the previous week, I'd just sat down and ignored everyone around me. But there was something very different that day. First of all, it was Monday, meaning my fellow students had their very first weekend at home with their parents after starting back to school. And that must have meant conversations about the new nigger kid from NYC.

My guess is that the animosity toward me stemmed from the parents' orientation event. Those ignorant parents who objected to a union like that of my parents – an ignorance of which there was plenty of in Ashford – had obviously used the weekend to push their warped bigotry onto their children; just like their *grand pappies* and their *great grand pappies* had done before them.

When I sat myself down to eat at a table I'd picked out randomly, a trio of boys and one plump, ginger-haired girl told me to go sit somewhere else. Getting up to leave, tray in hand, I noticed almost every single student within proximity of an empty seat was looking in my direction; I felt like a goddamned freak in a carnival.

Facing all those icy stares, I didn't have the guts to attempt to sit in an empty chair, so I had no idea what I was going to do next. Holding a tray containing a cheeseburger, limp fries, and a small carton of chocolate milk made me feel even more vulnerable – like the only way to get out of the situation would be to throw my food away and stand facing the wall. Also, I hadn't mastered the art of eating while holding a tray while standing while feeling condescended.

Something about being degraded in that way feels far worse when nourishment is involved. I can't quite explain why, but that's how I've always felt. Maybe it was because of the number of times my parents put me down while I was stuffing french fries with extra ketchup in my mouth, tears streaming down my face as I chewed my food. Mom and Dad were the ones who constantly yelled and put me down, but I still had no choice but to eat their food to stay alive. It was always dinner when I felt the most vulnerable, and I came to realize it was why they chose that particular time to vent their frustrations on me.

Only one year prior, my parents had insulted me while calling me *goddamn failure* as we ate dinner as a family. It was because they'd spent time with the neighbors and their cute, ever-so-smart five-year-old daughter, who had apparently told them she wanted to be a doctor when she grew up.

While it was something I'd normally not say, since the neighbors' little girl had said it, aspiring to a career in medicine became my parents' new standard to determine if a young child had their priorities set right. Thus, I'd instantly become a failure for not wanting to follow that path, and Mom and Dad didn't quit letting me know as much as they did over rice and roast chicken. I cried as I chewed my food, my snot and tears adding extra salt to the roasted thigh and leg. They'd always choose dinner – or a ride in the car if they wanted to mix things up a little – to berate me, and I became quite used to it.

But the incident the year before where I was told I was a *goddamn failure* hit me the hardest.

In the lunchroom, just as I was entertaining the thought of throwing my food away and cutting my losses, something over in the corner hit my peripheral vision. There was a desk there, the kind we had in the classrooms. This one was leaned crazily to one side with the small table section halfway broken. Regardless, that sorry-looking, broken-down table looked like a golden throne to me at that moment.

I carried my lunch tray over to the table and sat myself down. Although so many of my fellow students gawked at me like some unusual zoo animal, I finally felt at peace. The broken desk had become my bubble, and nothing outside it really mattered.

About fifteen minutes later, just as I gulped down the last of my cheeseburger and chocolate milk, Mrs. Allen, one of the school hall monitors, walked over.

"Why on earth are you sitting at the broken desk?" she asked.

"I have nowhere else to sit, ma'am," I responded as politely as my parents had taught me.

"I can count at least five seats that are free," she pressed. "I saw you sit down earlier and then get up again. Seems like you did have a place to sit."

"They didn't want me sitting with them and told me to leave. Everyone else was looking at me," I told her. However, in my mind, I was actually saying, *Bitch, if you saw me sitting here for the past fifteen minutes, why didn't your bitch-ass come say anything earlier?* Perhaps not quite verbatim as my ten-year-old lexicon was still limited when it came to expletives, but thinking back, oh, how I wish I said that. Even if I had though, it wouldn't have sounded as bad as what the colossal bitch replied with.

"Well, maybe you shouldn't give them a reason to not like you," she growled before walking away.

And that was pretty much it.

Bitch.

And so, that lame, broken desk became my permanent seat, and that's where I sat every single day. As it became the norm, my peers quit paying me any mind – with one exception.

Mark was in the lunchroom. He didn't give me much trouble, and usually gave me plenty of space when I walked by. It was as if I had the most contagious of diseases and those extra three inches of space he afforded me in the hallway meant the difference between being infected and living a life ordained by the hand of God.

Normally, I'd have been on edge upon seeing Mark, but on that particular day, I was pleasantly distracted. I noticed a girl sitting a few seats away from Mark; I'd seen her before, but only in passing. There she was, large as life and only a few strides away, talking to someone across the table – I couldn't see who, because Brett's fat ass was in the way. The girl always looked pretty and normally wore overalls – but sometimes she'd wear a cute dress to school. She always wore her hair in a ponytail and had the cutest high-pitched voice I'd ever heard in my life. Indeed, my first impression of her was her looks and demeanor, but what else was there? I don't know of too many guys who ask for a diploma before becoming interested in a girl. That's just nature, I guess.

I found out later that her name was Claire.

Claire Owen.

Several times during lunch, Claire would take a second here, maybe a few seconds there, to glance over at me. To me, her eyes always seemed filled with sadness and I would catch a glimpse of empathy in her sweet face. I didn't think it was at all possible, but it appeared that Claire felt for me and my ostracization. Even so, she never took the initiative to come over to talk to me, but I saw in her eyes she felt terrible seeing me being the class outcast sitting at the broken desk in the corner.

***

It's not as if I didn't make attempts to join in with my classmates' conversations about music, sports, teachers loved and despised, or to find someone to walk with in the hallways. I tried joining some of the afterschool clubs – chess, the debate team, and I even gave the indoor soccer team my best shot. Unfortunately for me, to be an active part of any club meant some level of interaction with other kids, and not one of them wanted anything to do with me.

So, sadly, it was all to no avail – I'd been given the stigma of school pariah because of my parents' mixed-race marriage and my skin color, and it stuck to me like a bad stink.

And so, despite all my best efforts, I was forced to live my school life in solitude. I did my very best to complete the assignments I was given in class and then I'd go home.

I pretty much trained myself to exist in my own mind and make my imagination my best friend. That worked well, as long as no external stimuli disrupted my fabricated sensory input. But inevitably, there'd be the bad days when the intrusions into my safe little world were too much to ignore.

One such day, as I sat eating a corndog at the broken desk, Brett walked up beside me. I didn't notice him, not even in my peripheral vision, until it was too late…

Now, let's face it, a corndog can look pretty phallic, and eating it can appear rather like fellatio to the young, warped mind. Brett appeared just as I slipped the corndog in my mouth and, grabbing my hand, he forced the thing in and out in a crude emulation of the sex act. Brett managed three, maybe four, strokes before I realized what was happening and was able to stop him.

It was too late.

Brett cracked up laughing, along with all the other kids in the lunchroom, before sitting back down with a dumb smirk on his stupid face.

I tried my best to ignore it, but I guess everybody has their breaking point. I hadn't reached mine, but I was getting pretty damn close. Opening the door of the sanctuary of my mind, I entered, and quickly I forgot I'd just been forced to blow a corndog in front of my entire grade.

Then, Brett threw a piece of cut fruit at me.

The irony was that ugly fuck wouldn't be caught dead eating any kind of fruit, so it was kinda funny he'd finally found a use for that perfectly cubed piece of pineapple. While I wouldn't consider my subsequent actions to the fruit assault to represent the full unleashing of my wrath, I shall admit a limit was reached.

I picked up the cupcake from my compartmentalized lunch tray and threatened to throw it at Brett with a simple gesture, a lift of the hand containing said dessert. Sadly, I was too chicken to follow through and I never actually threw the cupcake at my tormentor. Unlike throwing a small cube of pineapple, I knew better than launch a cupcake; they are large and would leave evidence in the way of spattered vanilla frosting. So, I put my cupcake back down and tried to finish my lunch. The short scuffle between Brett and I caught the attention of Mrs. Allen.

Slowly, she stood up from her seat and made her way over.

"What's going on here?" she demanded.

Although she only looked at Brett for an answer, I decided to chime in. "Brett was throwing food at me, Miss!"

"Ishmael, you will only speak when I speak to you, do you understand?" She silenced me with a stern wag of her finger. "Now, Brett, tell me what happened."

"Mrs. Allen, we were all sitting here by ourselves and not bothering no one when *Pissmael* threw some of his cupcake *at us!*" Brett's voice rose at the end, as if to add emphasis to his supposed distress.

"Don't call me that!" I screamed at the fat kid. "And I didn't throw anything!" I couldn't believe how easily that little motherfucker could lie through his teeth like that. Did they teach him nothing in Sunday School?

"Ishmael, don't get so worked up over stupid name-calling." Mrs. Allen snapped at me. "It's just a name. It won't kill you. You threw food at Brett?"

"No!"

"Yes, he did!" yelled Brett. "The cupcake almost hit me in the head!"

What came next was shocking to me. Every single student at Brett's table spoke up and claimed I'd almost hit all of them in the head with the cupcake. Even some of the kids at the adjacent table offered their worthless two cents.

"Is that right Ishmael?" said Mrs. Allen. "You had better come with me. And bring your lunch with you."

"No. I am not hungry anymore." I grumbled, standing up. "And I didn't do it!"

"Well, everyone here says you did. So, you're coming with me!"

It was a harsh learning moment for me: it was glaringly obvious I'd not thrown my cupcake – or any part of it – at anyone. The fucking thing was still on my tray! Mrs. Allen had simply *chosen* not to see it and side with my bullies.

And that hurt.

Despite my protestations of innocence, Mrs. Allen led me to the teacher's lounge. Since I'd left my lunch behind, she told me just to sit down until lunch was over – and that's exactly what I did. There were about twenty minutes of lunchtime left, and I used that time to reflect by staring at the white-painted brick wall at the far end of the lounge.

I guess I should have spent time reflecting on the injustice I'd been served and enjoying fantasies about fucking Brett up in the playground, but preserving my self-respect by dreaming of inflicting violence on my oppressors was a luxury I couldn't afford. Instead, I sat there and thought about how the whole sorry tale would be twisted by Mrs. Allen as she informed my parents, and their wrath once I got home.

Two minutes in, Mrs. Allen reappeared.

"I have to go back to the lunchroom," she growled at me, her breath rank with stale coffee and something I couldn't quite place. "You just sit here and think about what you've done."

I was furious, but I nonetheless accepted I couldn't control the situation and I had to be patient. It was just a feeling, nothing more, but enough to tell me my day would come.

So, I stared at that bland wall and thought about Claire. *My* Claire.

She was just so pretty, and given the opportunity, I knew we could have been something truly special. Sadly, I knew such an opportunity was unlikely to ever come at that school, but if it did, I wouldn't throw it away.

As I stared at the white paint, I noticed a dark blue binder on one of the countertops, leaning against the wall. Written on the binder's spine of the binder was: "locker list." Next to it sat a pen and a bottle of Tip-Ex correction fluid. Now that I think about it, I'm not sure how that brand made it to Ohio. Maybe somebody had brought it from overseas? Regardless, in a deduction that would have made Sherlock Holmes proud, I reckoned a locker change was on the horizon.

Adrenaline pumped through my veins.

If I had the opportunity, I wouldn't waste it. I'd make Claire my girl – forever.

Considering those previous thoughts, I wondered if Claire should be the only thing with which I would never waste an opportunity…

I had *opportunity* right there in front of me.

However, bad timing could ruin my entire school year and land me in the hottest water imaginable with my parents – even more than the false accusation of cupcake-throwing. I normally erred on the side of caution; after all, it was not even ten minutes ago when I'd been too shit-scared to throw the cupcake. But, the ease at which those other kids lied about me had gotten to me.

I had to do something.

I knew what I was planning would be risky, but nobody ever said risk couldn't be *calculated*. I'd been ordered to stay in the lounge, but Mrs. Allen didn't say I wasn't allowed to go take a shit – denying toilet breaks to kids was unlikely.

So, I got up and walked into the hallway; if anyone was to question me, I'd just say I needed the bathroom. In reality, I was scoping out the hallway outside the lounge to see if anybody was close by.

My luck was in.

Nobody at all.

Ducking back into the teachers' lounge, I opened the binder, which was organized by grade. I quickly found the fifth grade and found Brett's name: *Brett Abernathy. Locker 48. combination 18-6-2.*

I heard somebody coming – it was Mrs. Allen. I recognized those heavy, clumping footsteps anywhere. I shut the binder quietly and dashed back to where she'd told me to stay. But she walked in before I could sit down.

"What were you doing?" she demanded, her harsh voice garnering attention from everyone within earshot

I had to think fast.

"I need to use the bathroom, Mrs. Allen. It hurts to sit down, so I was standing up." I lied.

The ugly mammoth actually rolled her eyes in annoyance. "Go to the bathroom, Ishmael."

Leaving the lounge, I walked over to the bathroom and locked myself in one of the stalls. I didn't have to use the restroom, of course, but I wasn't entirely convinced Mrs. Allen wouldn't just walk in to make sure I was *really* shitting. Somebody was in the stall next to me; by the rotten smell emanating from that direction, they were having an especially bad day.

I walked out to find Mrs. Allen waiting outside.

"I didn't hear a flush," she snarled.

I had no idea what to say; she'd taken me totally by surprise.

I stood there in silence.

Even with her vindictive personality and obvious lack of intelligence, she must have known she'd crossed a line.

She ushered me back to the teachers' lounge and back to my seat facing the wall. I didn't mind – I'd gotten everything I needed. Mrs. Allen sat down behind me with the definite air of *waiting*.

A few minutes later, Principal Labar came in to the lounge and approached Mrs. Allen.

"Brenda, why is *he* in here?" he said softly so I couldn't hear. I could hear enough.

"He couldn't get along with the other students so he needed to be removed." I found her response odd: no mention of the supposed cupcake throwing? Maybe, given that the cake that had never left my tray had apparently hit twenty students without leaving a trace was too much for her lying ass to explain? Naturally, she left that part out.

"He doesn't need to be in here –and you need to take your shot. Are you ready?" he asked Mrs. Allen.

"Yes. I am. Ishmael, get out." The woman snapped at me as if I *wanted* to be there!

As I got up to leave, wondering what the hell a *shot* was, I heard Principal Labar scolding Mrs. Allen for talking to me like that. Entering the hallway, I made out bits and pieces of information: Mrs. Allen apologized and I heard *blood sugar* and *shot* by means of justifying her shitty attitude.

Even without understanding, the snippet stuck in my brain.

Lunch was almost over, so I decided to head back to the classroom. Some of the students that almost got hit with the imaginary cupcake smirked at me as I walked by, but I was at peace. I knew that prick Brett's locker combination, and all I needed was the perfect opportunity to unleash my plan.

Part I: Chapter Three

It didn't take me long to realize Brett and Mark were going to play a major part of my school experience in Ashford. Their cruel influence inevitably spread to some of the girls; in particular, I'll never forget Erin and Kristi. They'd make fun of me in the hallway, spread the rumor I had a *really* small penis, and taunted me that the first girl I'd ever fuck would be my mom.

There was no point telling on them: I knew not one single school official would ever believe me. The two girls were just so cute and innocent-looking; I'd often bear witness to them getting extensions on their homework assignments just because they claimed to have had *girl's problems* the night before – whatever that was supposed to mean. So, if they said I had a tiny penis and the whole school believed them, I just had to accept that.

My life at home wasn't that much better. My father always worked late and wasn't involved with anything me or Sarah did when he came home. And, when he was home, he'd snap at us both as if we were nuisances in our own home, and find things – *anything* – to shout at us for. Whether it was homework, grades, not doing our chores to some impossible standard he never shared, or simply to vent his anger and frustration, my father would berate and belittle us at every opportunity. On his good days, he'd just park himself in front of the television to watch the game and only barked orders and scream at us during the commercial breaks.

Always unapologetic, Dad would justify his abusive treatment of his own children as character-building.

One evening, about a month into the school year, I went downstairs for dinner. As usual, we weren't eating together – it was just my sister and me at the kitchen counter while my parents watched the news in the lounge. They sat glued to it religiously every night as if the world would end if they didn't keep up with everything going on in it.

I was still having trouble at school and I decided it was time to tell them about it. I approached my father, but before I could even speak, he held up his hand. I'd forgot the cardinal rule: only speak during the commercials.

So, I waited for another eight minutes before daring to speak.

"What? *What?* Speak up, boy!" my father snapped at me.

"I am having trouble at school, Dad. Some of the kids are picking on me."

"That's a normal part of school, you idiot," my father laughed. "Just man up and don't let them get to you."

"I am *trying*," I whined. "But they tease me *all* the time and it makes me sad and angry. Sometimes I can't study."

That angered my father. His face reddened; his jaw tightened. "You need to get it through your stupid head how important studying is? I didn't send you to that school to mix with degenerates who distract you!"

"You don't understand!" I dared to raise my voice. "They *lie* about me to get me into trouble!"

"I don't fucking care!" It was not often my father swore, but when he did, it was a clear sign he was well and truly pissed. "Do they live in this house? Do I have to take care of them? They don't live here so they don't matter a damn, you

dumb, ignorant boy! You are to behave at school and not do anything to disturb the hardworking school staff! *Anything*! Do you understand me, boy?"

"But they follow me around and…"

"Then go somewhere else, you whining little pussy!" Dad's eyes flicked to the TV; the news was about to come back on. "Is it too difficult for you to go where they don't see you?! All I ask you to do is go to school, pay attention, and get good grades – it's not much to ask, is it?"

Fighting back the tears, I shook my head.

"Are these other kids stopping you from doing that?" News or not, my father was on a roll – he seemed to enjoy berating me even more than his precious TV. "Are they taking your books? No! They're doing nothing to stop you doing what's expected of you! And when you come home, your mother and me don't make you do chores – all the bills are paid and you have a roof over your fucking head, you ungrateful, lazy little pig!"

"Please, Dad, speak nicely to me."

An exaggerated roll of the eyes. "Sure thing, pussy. The next time you act like a horse's ass at school and come whining to me, I'll say nicely – *excuse me Ishmael, please go study and don't get in trouble* – how does that suit your stupid little sensibilities?"

"That's not what I meant." The tears flowed unchecked down my face. Then, the commercials ended and the news came back on.

My father looked back at the screen. "Quit crying, you little piece of shit. Go to your room – you don't deserve to eat tonight."

I walked away, hoping for some sympathy from my mother. When I looked at her, she responded by saying, "Any more life lessons for Sarah, you horrible little boy?"

It wasn't the first time they treated me like this, and it certainly wasn't the last, but I knew that when I needed protection, I would have to fend for myself.

I had none from my parents and nobody to love me.

That night's homework assignment for Mr. Janicek was multiplication tables from 1x1 to 12x12. I had to write out the answers for every single combination. Normally, I would have found it pretty easy. My method was to count by every digit in the form of a song. For example, counting by 5s sounded similar to a rodeo-type, honkey-tonk tune. *Yee Haw! Now we got a 5, a 10, and a 15, and a 20, 25, 30, 35, 40, 45, and giddyuppin 50!* Counting by 7s sounded like a depressing love song or maybe even a lullaby. *Oh, 7, 14, 21, 28, 35! And 42, 49, and don't forget 56, and 63! And we will end our time together, with ol' 70!* However, my favorite was counting by 6s. It was suspenseful because the tune made it feel like it's impossible to know what's coming next. *Well, 6, 12, 18, 24, 30?... 36! Well, 6, 12, 18, 24, 30?... 36... 42!* And on it went until it hit 60.

However, no number of tunes could cheer up how I felt that night. I'd once again been placed in a subservient position to the television news, cussed out for having human emotions, and mocked for asking for some respect from my father. I didn't possess any motivation to do the best I could, because I had been made to feel like I was a piece of shit.

So, I filled out every answer from memory and called it a night.

***

The next day I turned in the assignment and sat through class in the back by the window. I ate lunch alone again and managed to stay sane until the end of the day – just about.

When I got home, I went straight to my room and listened to rap music; that night it was LL Cool J. It was the only outlet I had living in an emotionless home where I didn't seem to exist except to be yelled at.

Life had been like that pretty much for as long as I could remember. In contrast, my class back in New York City was incredibly diverse, so I didn't stand out as the only nigger in the room and there wasn't much to get in the way of having friends and doing well in school.

Schooling had always come easy to me – so my parents had no *real* reason to get angry and abuse me both verbally and physically. Yeah, they'd hit me plenty times – and oftentimes for the most stupid, miniscule reasons. Sadly, inevitably, over time, I'd grown accustomed to it and it just didn't affect me anymore. It didn't serve as negative reinforcement not to get things wrong – no, it was just a part of my crappy life I had to learn to live with. It was the same routine: wake up in the morning, and by nightfall, there'd be some reason to be hit, slapped, spanked, or called a *piece of shit*. After so long of being treated like that, I'd come to believe that's really what I was.

A piece of shit.

The night following my disastrous attempt to open up to my father, to garner his help with the relentless bullying I was receiving at school, I was called down for dinner. Once again, Sarah and I ate at the kitchen counter while my parents had their dinner in front of the television. Sarah was telling me about some show she liked and I'd pretty much tuned her out. It was some dumb little kids show with talking cartoon animals and clumsy moral codes – not the sort of thing I'd ever watch – but it was her absolute favorite, apparently.

In the middle of dinner, the phone rang and my father answered it. Obviously, I had no idea what the caller was saying, but somehow, I knew my grave was dug.

"Yes sir… Oh, is that *so*? Well, thank you for telling me. I assure you this will be handled swiftly… No, rest assured that you will see major changes from now on… Thank you, sir."

As I sat in my chair next to Sarah with fried rice still in my mouth, a huge dark shadow loomed over me. Looking up, I saw my father, face red, nostrils flared, huffing and puffing.

From the living room, one eye still on the TV, my mother looked concerned, frightened. "What's happened?" she asked my father.

"What happened on the multiplication homework, Ishmael?" Ignoring her, my father turned all his wrath onto me. "Mr. Janicek says you received a 65%? *A fucking 65%?* You got a fucking D in this house, you piece of fucking shit?" he screamed in my face, spittle raining down upon my cheeks.

"I didn't know, I'm sorry, *I didn't know*," I cried in desperation.

"Of course, you didn't know!" Dad raged. "Little shitty bastards like you don't know *anything*, do they? This whole week, when you were talking to your sister and watching television after school, didn't you *know* you had a math assignment?"

As a kid, answering a question like that is impossible.

"I didn't know he was going to assign it this week until he did it…" I managed to blurt out before a hard stinging slap across my face silenced me.

"Please don't hurt me!" I cried out, but to no avail. I knew the next sting of pain was on its way within seconds, and with it, the helpless feeling of knowing I could do nothing to stop it. All that, coupled with the fact it came from someone I was raised to believe loved and cared for me.

My father slapped me again.

Now my cries went from pitiful sobbing to a full-fledged scream of pain and anguish. I jumped from my chair and ran around the house screaming at the top of my voice as I tried to get away from my father.

"You stupid little boy! You lazy little bastard!" My mother hurled her own insults at me. "I wish you'd never been born, Ishmael – all you've ever done is cause this family trouble!"

"A fucking 65%! My father boomed over my mother's shrill tone, their voices blending into one to jab at my ears and my soul.

"Don't ever think we need you in this house!" Mom screamed as I ran upstairs. My father chased me, and then I was cornered in my room.

It was a stupid move on my part.

"Today you'll learn *something*, you little shit. Since you don't learn when I talk nicely, perhaps this will help."

He took off his belt.

Before my brain was able to anticipate what was to come, my father brought the belt down with a sharp *crack* on my arm. I saw the top layer of skin had shredded off to expose raw, bleeding flesh. Hot, searing pain burned through my arm as I dropped down to the ground. I knew I was screaming, my throat hurt like hell, but it was like hearing someone else's cries from afar.

Looking up, I saw him raise the belt again.

"No! Please don't… *please stop*! I love you so much!" I cried out. Of course, my fake display of affection didn't stop him – it never did.

He brought the belt down again.

I hardly felt it. I was on the floor, my senses fading in and out, tears and snot soaking into my carpet. And, despite the numbing of my senses, I heard clearly what my father said to me next, and I'd never forget it…

"Did you *love* that – you piece of *shit*!?"

I wasn't to know it at the time, but a part of my heart was permanently blackened that day. It was not the first time I'd been insulted, degraded, and beaten, but my father's words caused the worst pain I'd ever experienced – the vicious mockery of the affection I'd tried to display for him.

The belt lowered again.

"Get up, boy," my father snarled. "Go to the bathroom, clean yourself up, and do those *multiplication cycles* – properly this time."

Your guess is as good as mine as to what a multiplication "cycle" was supposed to be, but the fact that my father often mispronounced or misused common phrases when he was angry said a lot about his character: he literally couldn't think straight when anger took him over.

I managed to stand up and walk over to the restroom. My right arm was bleeding; the blood wasn't exactly flowing, but looked more like a gentle mist on the raw blister on my arm. I washed myself off and dabbed away the blood – it's amazing how quickly the soft and tender skin of a ten-year-old quits bleeding and starts the healing process. After I dried myself off, the blood welled up a little. I saw no point of getting rid of it. It was a part of me now.

After finishing my multiplication tables in what was an absolute waste of time – I'd already gotten that D, and redoing it wouldn't improve my grade – I started on my actual homework close to 9 p.m. I went to bed tired and, an hour and a half later, wasn't able to fully concentrate in class the next day. The cycle repeats itself, but as long as they had violent video games, profane music, and other kids to point the finger at, my parents would never be so humble as to blame my failings on themselves.

That night, as I laid down in bed and prepared to fade away, I remembered I'd forgotten to visit Sarah's room to tell her our nightly joke and kiss her to bed. She relied on it every night and was always ready for me when I went into her room. I wouldn't be caught dead breaking her heart by not doing so.

That night was different.

As I got up to go to her room, I stopped myself and laid back down. "Those jokes are fucking stupid, and I don't need to hang out with my stupid little sister," I thought to myself before falling into a deep and restless sleep.

Part I: Chapter Four

At school as at home, the insults and cruel bullying and teasing from my classmates carried on as usual. What made it worse was the teachers saw what was happening, but chose to look the other way. As sad as it was for me to admit, I honestly felt like the class was actually better off having me there. Having a common enemy, or in this case, a collective toilet for everyone to shit in, seemed to be good for the class's emotional regulation.

I looked different and was bred different, so naturally I was their *Chosen One*.

One day, Mr. Janicek informed us he intended to start each Monday's class with a show-and-tell session. We'd not have time for every student to participate every Monday, so Mr. Janicek decided to randomly select seven students each week. I wasn't chosen during the first week, and neither was my nemesis, Brett. To be honest, I really didn't pay much mind to which kids were chosen, but two did catch my attention: my secret crush, Claire, and that colossal prick, Mark.

Mark's presentation bored me, since it was about a Cleveland Indians baseball card and I was not really into sports, since it's shit I couldn't control. However, I did pay extra-special attention to Claire.

She'd brought in a diary her grandmother had given her. It had a built-in clamp that locked and had its own special silver key; I'd never seen a locking mechanism on a bound book before, so for show-and-tell, I found it most enlightening, even if the rest of the class appeared disinterested in the whole thing. What piqued my interest about it was the diary was obviously very precious to Claire, and it made me wonder if the rest of the class considered the presentations as an opportunity to bring personal things to school.

It was at that point I decided to pay that extra attention.

Erin was next. Erin, the spiteful little snake who liked to tell everyone my first sexual experience would be incestuous because I was a shitty, ugly person, walked up in front of the class clutching a small bag. What she pulled out glimmered and shone under the classroom's humming florescent lights. As much as I had little interest in finding out what she'd brought in, I did have a slight curiosity – but for nefarious reasons…

It was a bright blue, bedazzled hairbrush. Its handle was made from clear glass, its head outlined with a rainbow of colored rhinestones and shiny plastic jewels.

"This is my hairbrush that my Aunt Stacey gave me when I was little," Erin declared proudly. "I use it every day because Aunt Stacey is really, *really* special to me! I'm sorry, but I am not supposed to pass it around."

"That's really special!" said Mr. Janicek. "Thanks for bringing it in to show us, Erin."

As Erin sat back down, I was angry at how easily she passed herself off as an innocent angel in front of the teachers, yet was happy to verbally abuse me in the hallways. Lucky for me though, because I'd learned something about the little bitch: she had the ability to *feel*, and she really, *really* loved that hairbrush!

During lunch, I sat alone at my broken desk. The menu that day was cheeseburgers and fries with a vegetable side – a small array of limp, tasteless green beans; it was all incredibly disgusting. The only way I could force myself to eat that slop was by telling myself some kids in the world don't eat much at all, and to them my revolting school lunch would look like a feast. I guess it was the inherent guilt my parents instilled in me over everything – I was even doing it to myself! And so, I scarfed it all down and thanked God for it afterwards.

Just as I was opening my juice box, Erin and Kristi walked by me. As they did so, another insult was tossed my way.

"Hey *Pissmael*, why don't you go play with yourself?" Erin taunted.

The boys at the nearest table heard and immediately began their usual hooting and hollering – they sounded more like wild monkeys than human beings.

"Ohhhhh damn! Piss got told! Ohhhhhh! Ahhhh Sheee-yit," they cried out, as if what Erin had said was simply the wittiest thing ever.

"Don't call me that!" I yelled at my tormentor – that name was the one sure-fire way to elicit an angry response from me, and the evil little cow knew it.

Erin, without hesitation, turned her head towards Mrs. Allen and yelled back at me. "Don't you ever yell at me, Ishmael!"

Predictably, she lumbered over to investigate the grave injustice I'd meted out at poor, precious Erin.

"What's going on here?" she demanded, her words emphasized with a belch.

"Ishmael yelled at me!" Erin sobbed.

"She called me *Pissmael* and said gross things!" In that instant, I realized I really shouldn't have said that: up until that point, nobody had ever heard *me* say *Pissmael*.

It was like adding fuel to a hungry fire.

"Boys, calm down," Mrs. Allen barked. "You need to watch yourself, Ishmael. You need to stop making up stories. One more, and you go back to the teacher's lounge. Do you understand?"

"Yes ma'am."

She gave me another stern look and waddled away; I still couldn't believe she was able to hoist her fat bulk out of bed every morning.

***

That night was rather uneventful, which in the context of my home, I actually considered to be a very good night.

We had dinner and afterwards, I went upstairs to mind my own business. I had no means by which to play music in my room because my father had taken away anything he considered *recreation*. The slapping and belt whipping was never enough for him and my mother – physical pain was never enough for them unless laced with insults and garnished with the loss of any external stimuli that might possibly help me escape from my miserable reality. What my parents thought of as discipline, others would consider psychological torture.

As much as sitting in a desolate room sucked ass, that became a monumental night for me; it marked the first time I developed a more effective way to control how my mind conjured up its own escape – given my failure to live in my own mind during the corndog and pineapple incident.

Sitting on my bed, I stared around my room with such an empty mind I imagined I saw the dimensions of time and space. Visualizing the area my room took up in the universe, I figured it would change because our planet moved through the cosmos. The thought intrigued me.

Then, suddenly, I was standing on a vast stage playing an electric guitar. I had no idea *what* I was playing, but the song was so hard and sparks flew from the amp's cable. I sang into the microphone as I played, and thousands of adoring fans jumped up and down as I performed for them. I was a superstar, beloved and cherished by all my fans.

Strangely, though, I was rapping – even though I was quite clearly in a rock band.

After the set was done, the encore finished, my imagination shifted once more, and I was in a park and holding hands with Claire, the most beautiful girl I'd ever seen; we hugged tightly under a tall, verdant tree –my young, innocent mind wasn't quite ready to imagine kissing her, let alone anything else.

That was the first time I think I realized I was in love with Claire. It was also the first time I knew I could survive in my own mind when there were no physical, external stimuli to interrupt my thoughts. My mind had become a limitless, forever expanding universe, and I'd just discovered the key to imaginary travel anywhere in the universe – although it would be many years before I learned the term *astral projection*.

And, best of all, the feelings felt… *real*.

My thoughts soon returned to reality, and I found myself thinking back to the day's altercation in the lunchroom.

Erin's part in particular.

I'd decided to imagine her stupid face and even more stupid voice as my neighbor's dog – the dog that barked at me every time I went outside. I imagined he was saying, *Fuck you, you stupid mixed-race mutt! Eat shit, yo!* – but all I heard was, *bark, bark, bark*.

Eureka!

Erin no longer insulting me – that nasty little girl was just *barking* at me. In my mind, she was a bitch and hiding six titties under her sweater. I also told myself she probably preferred incestuous insults because she was inbred herself. So, the next time she dissed me, I'd simply think of her as a mangy Golden Retriever that eats its own shit and gets humped by her own brother, and all will be well.

Doing the mental gymnastics was quite relieving, and my mind soon turned to the phantom cupcake incident with Brett and his cohorts. Although I could reduce some of the insults to the barking of dogs or squealing of pigs, their situation was completely different. Of course, I couldn't shut off my skin to being receptive to the external stimuli of being forced to orally pleasure a corndog or feel the warm, wet embrace of a sugary pineapple hitting it, but I figured I could maybe train my brain to perceive all of that as simple background noise – I wouldn't walk into the ocean and then bitch that it's too wet, would I?

And yes, that's is how I rationalized things at the tender age of ten.

I found it to be a neat feeling to be a secret intellectual at that age, and while I could never condone any of the racist treatment I was subjected to, I had discovered a silver lining. No one expected me to be smart, so whatever I decided to do to them, they'd never see it coming. I was the humble mosquito: too insignificant to notice – right up until the moment it injects you with malaria.

And that made things so much easier.

Part I: Chapter Five

It was close to three months before anyone in Ashford really interacted with Jadrich Lima outside the everyday courteousness at the grocery store or post office. Whenever he was seen in such places, he'd extend simple pleasantries before making a hasty retreat. I discovered that first-hand because my parents ran into him at the hardware store one day. Lima was actually one of the few folks who didn't give my parents the cold shoulder, and that stuck with me.

I recall one day, shortly after exchanging nods and hellos with Lima at the store, my parents telling me and Sarah about the strange new religious man in town.

"So, as it turns out, he seems like a decent man, albeit very odd," said Dad.

"How is he odd?" I asked.

"He's not like the rest of the people in Ashford," my father explained. "He seems kind and doesn't care about how people are different – he doesn't judge at all, at least from what I can tell."

"What was he buying at the hardware store?" I was intrigued.

"Aren't we inquisitive today? Well, I have a feeling the local Church will open soon." He dodged my question.

"How do you know that?"

"Yeah, how you know, Daddy?" My little sister joined in.

"Because I saw –"

"No, Samuel, let the boy figure it out," Mother interrupted.

"Okay, tell me, Ishmael." My father stared straight into my eyes. "I saw him buying restroom signs. What does that tell you?"

"I've seen construction trucks in front of the church," I told him. "So, if he's buying restroom signs, then whatever he's doing with the church is almost finished."

"How so, Son?"

"Because those signs would be last."

"Good job, Ishmael." Mom actually sounded pleased with me!

"I have a question," I added.

"Yes?" Dad raised an eyebrow.

"What did you mean when you said he's not like the rest of the people here?" I ventured.

"Well, umm, some people in this town like things a certain way and think different things are bad for them," Dad replied.

"Are *we* different?" asked Sarah.

"I don't think so," our father told her. "But I think many people do. We just have to work hard to make sure they know we are good people."

"Is it because Mom is black?" I asked.

"Ishmael, you shitty little –"

"Samuel!" Mom snapped. "Don't start this again!"

"No, no, no… it's not because your mom is black." Dad's face gave away his lie. "People are just rude, that's all." I knew his answer was an insult to my intelligence.

"Sometimes in school, the kids call me *nigger*, and the teacher doesn't say anything," I told them.

"What did I tell you about hanging around those kids?" Dad was getting angry.

"I don't," I protested – as if I'd ever deliberately hang with kids who called me that. "They find ways to get to me, though."

"Stop brushing him off, Samuel," Mom chipped in.

"I know what you mean, son." Dad softened a tad. "Some people at work say similar things about me for loving your mom – behind my back, because grown-ups are like that. But I have to let it roll off me or I wouldn't have a job for long."

"Oh."

"That's why I need you to stay in your books. That's your only way out," Dad said.

"What a *nibber*?" Sarah piped up – I'll never forget how that terrible word sounded coming from the lips of a four-year-old.

"See what you did, you stupid, shitty little kid?!" My father pointed at my sister who was beginning to cry.

"I didn't do anything!" I protested loudly. "I was just telling you about school!"

"In front of your fucking sister!" he screamed at me.

"Well, you call me *shitty* in front of her!" I cried. My retort was infallible; Dad raised his hand, threatening to strike me.

"Mom! I didn't do anything wrong!"

"Quit whining, Ishmael," Mom dismissed me. Her frustration was clearly in response to the situation and not me personally. I felt abandoned regardless.

"Go upstairs! Git! *GIT*!" Dad's scream hurt my ears, but at least he'd not brought that fearsome fist down.

I ran upstairs and slammed my bedroom door shut.

From downstairs, I heard Sarah's cries. It seemed like the longer I existed, the more I angered everyone around me. I was losing my sense of apathy and beginning to see life as a game of survival. In war, one needs a good defense and offense. I had my defense, thanks to my newfound mental dexterity, and all I needed was a good offense.

About a half hour later, I ventured back downstairs because I was still hungry.

"Why are you back down here, Ishmael?" Dad growled. The TV was on and thankfully I only got a fraction of his attention.

"I didn't finish my dinner," I told him.

"Microwave it if you need to – but be quick."

I did just that and sat at the table alone, eating my too-hot dinner with my head down.

Mom joined me, probably out of guilt.

"Mom? I have a question."

"You do?" she replied.

"What's *blood sugar* mean?"

Part I: Chapter Six

My father was right.

A week after the conversation about Jadrich Lima at the hardware store, the Church reopened. Only, it was no longer called the Church of Ashford. The sign outside, covered by a tarp until the big day one dull Friday afternoon, shone like a beacon when unveiled.

The Ashford Association of Patriots

As we drove by, on our way out to dinner, my father, mother, sister, and I saw Jadrich Lima sitting outside the church on an old wooden table. He wasn't making any attempt to entice people to speak to him: no megaphone, no sign, absolutely nothing. But there was something in the way he sat there out in the open, smiling warmly at passersby that felt welcoming – as if he was just *hoping* for someone to stop and talk.

The man's patience was divine, but also intriguing: even I wanted to stop the car to see what it was all about. I noticed a few people were already approaching him.

My mother told Dad to pull over; I think she just wanted in on whatever was going on.

Exiting the car, the four of us headed toward the line to see Jadrich Lima. As we approached, the middle-aged couple in front of us took a few steps forward to create distance between them and my mother – like Mom carried Ebola or something.

Undeterred, my mom maintained her dignity with nothing more than an eye roll.

Finally, it came our turn to meet Jadrich Lima. As we walked up to him, his attention was squarely on my father. He didn't even acknowledge me, Sarah, or Mom.

Standing up, Lima extended his hand towards my father. "Well, hello, sir. Good to see you again!"

"Same to you, Mr. Lima," my father replied, shaking the man's hand.

"Dial it back now, *Mr. Lima* is what they call my father." Lima gave Dad the broadest smile. "Call me Jadrich. And you are…?"

"Samuel. And this is my wife, Madilyn, my son, Ishmael, and my daughter, Sarah."

"Well, it's wonderful to meet you all," Lima declared with another grin.

"So… what's going on here?" asked my father.

"I'm here for the good people of Ashford." Lima swept a hand backward to indicate the church. "I believe Ashford folks are only the first of many chosen by a divine power. I am a man of God, but I think sources like the Bible and Torah need a more *divine* interpretation by those of a higher order and pre-selected by the Almighty. God told me to come to Ashford. This town is small, but I know the people are divine."

I couldn't help but notice Lima left out the Koran, which represented a faith just as Abrahamic as the others. Was that deliberate?

"So, is this a new religion?" asked my father.

"Oh no, not at all." Lima laughed. "The natural order of the Almighty can't be labeled as simply as *religion*. It just *is*.

It's as natural as the sky is blue or the grass is green. Why don't you take a pamphlet?" Lima handed my father a trifold pamphlet. Noticeably, he didn't offer one to my mother, or my sister and I. Quite the contrast from how my father described him from their interaction at the hardware store.

"Thank you." My father gave the pamphlet a cursory glance and we all left.

"Samuel, there is still hope for you. I believe in you!" Lima called after us.

Of course, I had no idea what he'd meant by that. And, when I did, I knew things would have been much better if I'd never figured it out.

Part I: Chapter Seven

A nd so, the rest of my school year continued along the theme set in those early days.

To this day, I still can't understand why schoolyard politics isn't offered as a PhD level discipline –

because it sure as fuck should be. If it was, kids like me might just stand a chance of surviving school with minimal psychological and emotional damage.

While those first few weeks of schoolyard horror began with Brett, Mark, Kristi, Erin, and a selection of the school's staff, over time – like some malignant, spreading disease – the collective delight of putting me down soon because the norm. Not one single day went by where I wasn't called *nigger*, *faggot*, or *Pissmael*, and the number of times I was told to go fuck my mom was countless.

Mr. Janicek and the hallway attendants loved to use me as an example to the other students, either by writing me up for something all the kids did without recourse or verbally scolding me while ignoring everyone else. I guess it was hard for them to discipline kids that resembled their own family, but luckily, they had us dark kids to pick on.

Over time, I became better and better at internalizing the abuse, but that did nothing to negate the pressure building up inside me; my still-forming mind had no vents with which to release that pressure. I was far too young to fuck bad bitches, smoke weed, snort a line of coke, or look at porn. Shit, I didn't have a Victoria's Secret catalog to ogle – my parents would never allow such a thing in our house.

It all made for an unbearable life.

Another typical Monday, another show-and-tell. That week was of particular interest to me because it was both Brett's turn and mine. There wasn't much I had to take to class, or at least not anything I wanted to show, knowing anything would make my classmates tease me further. So, I took along my favorite Star Wars bookmark. I was actually rather fond of the thing – it was made out of plastic and featured Darth Vader on both sides. His lightsaber beam was made out of red foil that glimmered and shone almost like the real thing.

My turn.

I walked to the front of the class, bookmark in hand. I hadn't expected much interest in it, and my expectations were confirmed. Half the students weren't paying attention, the other half were watching but looking for an excuse to mock me – hence I'd chosen the bookmark, and not something too personal, like, let's say, the birthday card Sarah made for me.

It was all done and over faster than I expected. Mr. Janicek had never set a minimum time limit on our presentations, so I was done in thirty seconds flat: *wham bam, thank you Ma'am*.

Walking back to my seat, I heard Mark make a quip to his crew.

"Bet he likes that lightsaber up his ass!" he said and they all snickered. Mr. Janicek heard him, but of course, didn't do much more than give a disapproving look.

As with Erin from the week before, I was interested in what Brett had brought with him to class: I hated the kid and no amount of knowledge could ever be too much.

Brett waddled his fat ass up to the class. He just stood there and didn't say a word. His face was expressionless, although it was obvious he had something up his sleeve.

"Brett, are we waiting on something for your show-and-tell?" asked Mr. Janicek.

"Nope!" said Brett. The ceremony of the moment was clear.

"Well, won't you begin?"

"Already did!" Brett grinned and looked down at his feet. "My show-and-tell are my shoes! I got them for my birthday last week from my mom and dad! I've wanted these Nikes for a long, long time!"

A bunch of kids, mostly the boys, stood up on their chairs to get a better view of Brett's feet, much to the fat kid's delight.

"Class," Mr. Janicek said. "How about we have Brett take a quick walk around so we can all see his new shoes. Go ahead, Brett."

Brett obliged with little reservation, and most of the class made an effort to look at his shoes; a few others simply turned their heads slightly – a token gesture.

I, for one, wasn't paying any attention to the fat idiot – I couldn't give a fuck about his shoes.

Lunch was peaceful that day. Mrs. Allen left me alone for once, and the other students didn't pay me any attention as I sat alone at my broken desk. I ate in peace and didn't have anything thrown at me. I guess you could say, it was a good day – I've always loved that song.

I took a little longer than the other kids to leave the lunch room; I was caught up in a book I was reading while eating and I was lost in its world. By the time I stood up to leave, most of others were either at their lockers or already in their classrooms.

However, one student was heading back towards the lunchroom; I recognized her beautiful silhouette immediately.

As she walked by, Claire looked toward me and said, "Hi Ishmael," with a gentle wave of her slender fingers. Her voice was loud enough for me to hear but not to travel down the hallway; it was as if her voice at that moment was only for me.

It was the first act of kindness ever bestowed upon me in Ashford, Ohio. Not only that, it was from Claire! First an uneventful lunch and now that!

"Hi," I replied, making a conscious effort to not look back as she left my sight – I didn't want to look too eager.

I was in a daze.

Aware I was walking toward my classroom, I didn't remember the journey. All I could think about was Claire. She'd actually taken the time to look at me. She'd waved at me. She'd said hi to me. But, most importantly of all, Claire had smiled at me.

She had looked so beautiful; her pigtails that went down to the base of her neck, the delicate necklace with the pink pendant… as I walked, I fell into the daydream about kissing Claire again. Nothing wild, just a gentle peck on the lips or smooth cheek would have sufficed. I was in ecstasy.

Sadly, my daydream fantasy didn't last long…

Out of nowhere, my head was slammed hard into a locker against the wall. The blow came out of nowhere and caught me completely off guard.

As the initial shock wore down, the pain throbbed through my head like a beating drum. I saw Brett standing next to me; he wasn't laughing, so I knew his intentions were based on principle.

"What the hell, Brett?" I grumbled in a barely coherent ramble. Looking around, I saw nobody around us.

"Shut up you stupid, dumb *nigger*," Brett snarled with vicious conviction.

"What did you just call me?" I was mad, seeing red mad.

"I said, shut up, *fag*. *Little pussy*," he replied.

"What is your fucking deal?" I growled at Brett. "And don't call me a pussy!"

"I hate *you people*." Brett looked down his nose at me, like I was the piece of shit my father always told me I was. "Just fuck off, okay? And we all know the first pussy you'll get is your mom's," he laughed as he walked away.

It sure does make one wonder how a kid would learn rhetoric like that at such a young age.

My anger bubbled over. Brett had physically assaulted me for no reason – but, even worse, he'd ruined my sweet mental moment with Claire. She was the only thing making me happy in that God-forsaken place, and he'd fucked it up.

I ran up behind Brett and pushed him in the back. It wasn't a hard push, but force is exacerbated when the recipient doesn't see it coming.

With a loud, surprised grunt, Brett stumbled forward and fell to his knees. I wish he'd fallen all the way. As a matter of fact, I wish I'd broken his fat, stupid neck.

I had no idea what I was going to do next, but I didn't have to think for long. I hadn't noticed Assistant Principal Penny Kells standing in the hallway twenty or so feet behind me.

"Ishmael!" she screamed.

I turned around to see the elegant, graceful woman running towards Brett as he picked himself up, her face a picture of concern.

"Ma'am, he started it!" I protested "He called me *nigger*!"

"All I saw was you pushing him," A.P. Kells replied. "Brett, are you okay, dear?"

"I guess so," Bret sniffled. "I don't know why he did that to me!"

"You called me a nigger!" I yelled in his fat, red face.

"Stop using that word!" A.P. Kells was angry at me for using the racial slur I'd been subjected to since the semester began – *angry at me!* "Brett, if you're okay, please go to class. Ishmael, you come with me!" She held out her arm to usher me away from Brett.

She took me to her office.

There, I saw pictures of her and her happy, smiling family on her desk, along with a handful on the bookshelves. It was remarkable how much her kids looked like so many of the students in the school – little shiny, smiling, white faces. I, on the other hand, must have looked like the color of shit to her, and therefore completely unrelatable.

As I sat quietly contemplating her sickly-sweet, white-skinned family, Principal Labar appeared and took me to his office with A.P. Kells. All attempts to defend myself were futile; after a brief call with my parents, I was suspended for three days.

As usual, when I got home, I got my ass beaten with Dad's belt and cursed out by both my parents well past midnight. Only that time, I didn't care; I knew I had no sanctuary at home or at school.

So, I took my belt whips and insults the best I could manage and went to bed, all ready to reboot when I woke up.

***

"They say they're people of God, but they couldn't be further from that if they tried. Those assholes," my father grumbled at the dinner table on my second day of suspension.

"Can't you get a transfer back to New York?" asked my mom.

"No, not until the contract ends," Dad replied with a scowl. "Until then, I guess we're stuck here. The added equity on the mortgage doesn't seem worth it anymore."

"Are we moving back to New York?" I chipped in.

"Shut up, Ishmael! Adults are talking. Just *shut up*!" Dad snapped at me.

I'd forgotten the cardinal rule of our house: *Just shut the fuck up*.

If I ever had something on my mind, save it. If I had something to tell them, wait until the commercials and hope I'd be allowed to speak. Sarah and I both knew our place, and for a second, I had completely forgotten. So, I shut my mouth and listened quietly.

"Samuel, did you talk to HR?" Mom wanted to know.

"Of course, I did!" Dad barked back. "But what goddamn good does that do when they're the same way? They are from here!"

"Maybe corporate?" she ventured.

"And give the bastards here a reason to say 'oh oops, you are fired! Sorry!'? I just can't risk it."

My parents fell silent, took a deep sigh, and continued their dinner. After a few mouthfuls, they turned on me.

"Ishmael, did you finish your homework?" asked Mom.

"Yes." I nodded for emphasis.

"Okay, start tonight on tomorrow's work," she added. "You're lucky Principal Labar sent it all home with you, so get a head start."

"But I finished *today's* work," I protested. "I'm supposed to go by the lesson plan."

"Oh, so you get suspended from school and now you want a break?" Mom mocked me. "Oh, *King* Ishmael, how can me and your father possibly make your life easier?"

"You don't have to make fun of me," I mumbled.

"And what *should* I do?" Mom's question was rhetorical, of course. "You got yourself suspended from school, and now I have to sit at home and look at you all day? Now, go upstairs and start on Mr. *Jenny Chock's* lesson!" She still couldn't say his name right.

"But... he said I was supposed to go day-by-day because when we get back, he's –"

A familiar sting spread across my face.

My father had slapped me.

Hard.

"Why did you do that?" I screamed, not caring about escalating his wrath.

"Why are *you* so resistant to school work, you little shit?" Dad growled back.

"I'm not, but my teacher said –"

Throwing my dinner plate down onto the floor, I ran upstairs to my room with food still in my mouth. My parents didn't follow me; I slammed the door and cried in my room.

If only they'd have listened, I could have explained that Mr. Janicek wanted a rundown of everything I did, day-by-day, while at home. Part of my assignment's rules were to complete things as they were assigned – I'd actually *lose* points for going ahead.

My parents' ideas were out of date and from *their* time at school, not mine.

As my flow of tears started to run dry, a gentle knock on the door sounded out before it opened. I didn't get a chance to acknowledge the knock, so it could have only been one person: Sarah walked into my room and sat next to me on the bed.

"Iss, are you okay?" she asked.

"I guess so."

"Are you hurt?"

"I was. It doesn't hurt anymore."

"Do you want cookies?" She smiled sweetly at me, warming my heart.

"Sure, I can take a cookie," I said. A cookie seemed pretty good at that moment.

"Umm, I *eated* the last Oreo. No more," she said.

"Ate," I corrected.

"What?"

"The word isn't '*eated*', its '*ate*.'" I told her. "Don't you remember, you silly duck?"

"Okay," Sarah said before walking out of my room. She never said goodbye when she left – it was one of the many things I loved about my little sister.

I sat there in my room and re-read the assignments I'd done earlier that day. Of course, I ran the risk of my parents asking to see what I was doing, but thankfully the TV was on.. That would be my salvation. That boob-tube had a higher status than me in our house, and in that instance, it served me well.

About 45 minutes later, during a commercial break, my father opened my bedroom door and came in to look at what I was doing. Then he left. I knew he wouldn't be back, and I had no idea what he was looking for. I had no means of entertainment in my room and he didn't look at my assignment. For all he knew, I could have been writing a love letter to Claire. He'd poked his head into my room as a display of dominance, it was as simple as that.

That Thursday, I returned to school following my suspension.

As it turned out, Brett was not suspended and had gotten away scot-free for calling me nigger, and I would have given up anything to see him served a little justice.

In the lunchroom, I sat at my usual desk. I chose not to eat – it was always a gamble as to whether I would be able to or have my food used to degrade me. So, I just sat quietly: no book, no comics, no homework. I didn't have jack shit with me. I just sat there and looked down at my desk and waited for the lunch bell to ring.

After a while, I had to use the restroom. I stood up and made my way across the hall. Not paying too much attention, I inadvertently took the route by Brett's and Mark's table.

"Hey *Pissmael*, did you fuck your mom when you were at home?" Mark taunted.

"Dude, just shut up!" I snapped back. I didn't dare follow up with an insult – that would have been repeated straight back to the colossal bitch that was Mrs. Allen.

As I kept on walking, something wet hit the back of my head.

One of them had thrown of a chunk of tuna sandwich at me. I knew it was Brett because he *always* ate the same sandwiches.

Prick.

I stepped out into the hallway, the only hallway we were allowed in during lunch, and went to the restroom. After peeing, I returned to the hallway and noticed Mr. Decker walking away from his post and towards the restroom. He walked with an odd gait, which led me to deduce he was holding in a major shit and wouldn't be back for quite some time. Strange he didn't use the teacher's lounge restroom. Maybe he had to go really bad. I really didn't know, but it would present a good opportunity for me. The other hall monitor, Ms. Simpson, was distracted by some giggling female students and wasn't looking in my direction at all.

Without thinking, I ducked out of view and made my way along the hallway. Of course, I ran the risk of someone seeing me, but life is not without its risks – I had to lay in wait with risk to taste glory.

Acting on pure instinct, I hurried down the deserted hallway and turned the corner at its end; fortuitously, it was the hallway that housed the lockers for my classroom. Stopping at the line of lockers, I listened intently for a second or so. Hearing nothing, I kept going until I reached locker forty-eight.

There, I heard footsteps.

I froze in panic and contemplated going to my own locker. Doing so would guarantee I'd be seen, but at least I'd have a good reason to be there. Or… if I remained perfectly still and prayed, just maybe I'd get out of my predicament. Hell, I'd already taken enough risks thus far, so I decided to go full-bore. The most my parents could do was kill me, and I wasn't scared of that anymore; I was convinced Sarah – the whole family for that matter– would be better without me, and thus I had nothing to lose.

The footsteps got louder and louder until the school janitor arrived at the hallway intersection. Luckily for me, he just kept on walking – he didn't as much as glance to the left where I was standing.

My prayers had been answered.

I walked up to locker forty-eight. I couldn't remember the combination right away, but recalled the trick that made it easier for me to memorize: adults and thirds. I didn't have much time to travel down the riddle road to remember the combination. One becomes an adult at 18. I always knew that fact because my mother brought it up often at home. It was the age she'd finally be rid of me. So, one third of eighteen is six. One third of six is two. The combination to locker forty-eight was 18-6-2.

Hell yeah!

Pausing, I listened one more time for footsteps. All was quiet. I was well-aware I'd been away from the lunchroom for only about three minutes, and knew my absence wouldn't draw suspicion for a while.

Finally, I opened the locker and peered in. I didn't know what I was looking for, but looking down I espied a shoebox with the Nike logo on it. I poked at the box and found it to be heavy; opening the lid, I saw Brett's precious shoes, the one's he'd so proudly shown off during show-and-tell.

I had no idea why Brett kept his shoes in a box in his locker and not on his feet or at home. Maybe he kept them for gym class, or to show off to his dumbass friends. The truth was, I didn't really give a fuck why; at that moment, it was nicely convenient for me.

Grabbing a pair of safety scissors from the top tray of Brett's locker, I cut both shoes' laces down the center. It was surprisingly harder than I thought – I'd expected the scissors to glide through those laces like a hot knife through butter, but they simply got stuck the harder I pushed. Nonetheless, the laces gave way to the blunt scissors slowly but surely. After I finished with the laces, I used the side of the scissors to slice a few gashes inside the leather sides of each shoe.

I'm not sure if that's how serial killers are born; I guess you can't compare destroying shoes to the murder and mutilation of small animals that seems to indicate future psychopaths, but it sure felt good ruining Brett's shoes. The scissor's blades going into the leather made me feel like I was cutting into Brett's fat, ugly face. It was good imagining slicing into his fucking skin – it's a pity shoes don't bleed.

Thirty seconds in and the damage was pretty good, although I felt it needed an extra push. So, I grabbed a red marker from Brett's art container, removed the cap, and ran its felt tip up and down the cuts I'd made in his precious Nikes – it was my *coup de grace*. That little shit had no hope of ever recovering his kicks.

Done. I quickly threw the marker back into the container, shut Brett's locker, and walked away as fast as I could.

I went back the same way I came and turned the corner back to the main hallway. Luckily, Mr. Decker still had not returned – it really must have been one hell of a shit!

Slipping back into the restroom, I returned to my stall and sat awhile making farting noises until I heard Mr. Decker flush his toilet.

Soon after Mr. Decker flushed we both exited our respective stalls at the same time. We washed our hands together, and he did nothing to acknowledge me. However, I couldn't risk him not remembering seeing me there – awkwardness would be a small price to pay.

"Hi, Mr. Decker!" I said.

"Hello, Ishmael." He eyed me with some disdain.

"Just washing my hands after using the restroom, ya know." I grinned at him.

"I would expect that from you, Ishmael," Mr. Decker replied with a quizzical look.

"I don't think I should touch things after wiping with toilet paper until I wash my hands!" I continued.

"Ishmael, that goes without saying. As in, it doesn't need to be said." Mr. Decker looked at me as if I'd gone quite mad.

"Okay, bye." I wiped my hands on my pants – the air hand dryers were less than efficient.

"Okay…" Mr. Decker watched me go with a slight shake of his head.

That couldn't have gone any better. It was weird and awkward, but more importantly, it had been unforgettable.

Thus, my alibi had been established.

The rest of the school day went on as normal, although my adrenaline rush of ripping into Brett's shoes gradually morphed into terror as the day progressed. I was still unsure as to what had sparked me to duck out into the hallway in the first place, but all of the subsequent events had happened automatically – as if I was being controlled by something else. Maybe that something else was my need for justice, or was it *revenge*? I had no idea, but planetary alignment was definitely calling the shots.

However, once my heinous crime was done and I was sitting in the classroom, the gravity of what I'd done hit me hard and I had a moment of clarity.

I looked over at Brett. I almost pitied him as he innocently sat there, intermittently paying attention to the lesson and doodling on his notepaper, with no idea what awaited him in his locker. He looked like any other, normal all-American boy sitting in a classroom, a poster child for American values. Yet, in my eyes, Brett might as well have been Lucifer himself; He was nothing more than the source of so much pain and suffering for me. That mommy's little angel was the devil to someone else, but no one knew it – except me and him. I hated Brett when he lashed out at me, but I hated him even more when he looked so ordinary and innocent.

A few hours later, the final bell rang. As usual, I hung back a few minutes to let the other kids catch their buses so I wouldn't be picked on in the parking lot. I walked home, which made sense as I only lived a third of a mile away. Plus, Brett, Mark, Erin, well, now I think about it, pretty much *everyone* bar a handful of kids rode the bus. I was alone when I walked and I liked that. The only other walker I cared about was Claire.

After ten minutes, Mr. Janicek noticed I was still in class.

"Ishmael, you can stay behind to get your work done, but I'm leaving in five minutes. You'll have to go to after-school study hall," he told me, and I thought he didn't sound like too much of an asshole.

"Okay, I might go there… or go home." I packed my stuff up and left the classroom to go my locker. As I turned the corner, I heard a commotion over by Brett's locker.

Shit.

My moment of truth had finally arrived. By the lockers, I saw Brett sobbing uncontrollably. Principal Labar was with him, and his ruined Nikes shoes lay on the floor between them.

They had nothing on me, and I knew that – but I still had to play it cool. My first instinct was to try to ignore what was going on, but I quickly let that idea go: a scene is a scene, and had to be treated like one.

As I neared Brett's locker, I figured it best to acknowledge what was going on. After all, I'd heard my mom and dad many times debate if not looking over at a cop next to them at the lights somehow looked more suspicious.

So, I walked by and looked over at Brett and the Principal. Pausing momentarily, I mouthed, *"Oh my God."*

Luckily for me, Principal Labar saw me. "Ishmael, none of this is your business. Keep walking," he said. Shrugging my shoulders without saying a word, I looked straight ahead and walked towards the exit.

They didn't suspect a damn thing.

Once outside, I made the left turn leading out to the street. It was then I noticed the shadow behind me. It became obvious it was approaching me. I turned around and was shocked to see Claire.

"Hi Ishmael!" she breezed.

"Oh, hi Claire."

"I wanted to say I liked your show-and-tell. I don't watch *Star Wars*, but I have a brother – so I know a little bit about it."

"Thanks! I like *Star Wars* a lot," I told her, hoping she'd walk with me awhile.

"Okay, bye!" she said with a wave.

"Bye." I hid my disappointment well – after all, Claire had made an effort to say hello a second time!

If there was a Heaven, that was surely it.

Part I: Chapter Eight

T he next day, my mother was to pick me up from school. As I sat waiting for her on the curb, I overheard a conversation between two students – both boys – sitting a few feet away. I didn't know their names, but I'd seen them in the hallway. They never gave me any trouble, and I'm pretty sure they were both in different grades.

"So, how come you weren't at the Church service last Sunday?"

"Where was it at?"

"Last week, I think it was at Mrs. Allen's house."

"From our school?"

"How many Mrs. Allens do we know?"

Listening intently, I couldn't help but wonder what a Church service at *her* house would look like.

"Oh, my parents wanted to try something different."

"Because there wasn't room last time? Last time it was cramped and smelled like ass."

"Nah, man. You heard of that Jadrich Lima guy?"

"Yeah, I saw him in front of the old Church. My parents never talked to him."

"My folks went to his service last Sunday."

"He has service on Sundays now? So, it *is* a Church or somethin'?"

"I don't know *what* that shit was. It was weird, though. I didn't pay attention."

"Gotcha. Maybe I'll tell my parents about it."

"Cool. And what's even more fucked up is the guy didn't talk about Jesus, God, or the Bible at all."

"Damn, man – my mom won't like that."

"Well, there were only four other people there, and they were into it."

"Okay, oh shit… hey, my mom's here. Peace."

"Later."

And with that, the first boy left.

I remembered meeting Jadrich Lima the day my whole family stopped off to see him. My mom certainly didn't seem to like him, but I'm not sure how Dad felt.

A few minutes later, Mom showed up. I walked over the to the car and climbed in. Sarah was already there; she immediately leaned over her car seat to give me a hug.

"Hi, Duck," I said.

"Hi Iss." She greeted me with a broad grin.

"Are you happy to see me?" I teased.

"No!" she said. My little sister always refused to admit affection, though she was able to show it in spades.

"How was school, Ishmael?" asked Mom.

"Good."

"Are you keeping out of trouble and not pushing any more kids over?" Weird question. If I'd done it again, she'd have been the first to know. It was always the same with my parents, though, and I was used to it: any wrongdoing or deviation from perfect behavior that inconvenienced them would linger forever like a poison cloud refusing to dissipate.

Forgiveness and redemption were luxuries my parents didn't afford me.

"Yes." I said.

"Okay, good."

"Hey, Mom? I have a question," I said.

"If you have a question, boy, then just ask." she snapped. I hated it when she spoke to me like that.

"Remember that Jadrich Lima guy?"

"Yes."

"Is the building he bought still a Church?"

"Ishmael, did you see me ask him?" Mom's tone was most curt. "Did he walk up and tell me what he has done with the building? Am I involved in his life? Don't you *ever* think before asking stupid questions?"

"I don't know if you know the answer. I was only asking," I said.

"Well, I *don't* know."

"Okay."

I fell silent.

In life, many people become acquainted with the phrase *you don't know what you don't know*. That wasn't a concept for my mother. If I asked her a question she knew the answer to, she'd tell me. However, if she *didn't* know, she'd always put the blame on whomever asked the question as if it was the dumbest thing ever asked. She even did it to my father on numerous occasions, and I'm pretty damn sure he found it irritating, though he didn't really say much about it.

"Some kids in school were talking about it and their parents went there. Are we going to also?" I broke my silence.

"You can ask your father, but I would say we *won't* be going."

"Why not?" I asked.

"Ishmael, don't harass me! I don't know!" She raised her voice, which was my cue to shut up.

I took the hint.

Part I: Chapter Nine

I always liked to think of myself as a good person who cares for others. I like to think of myself as one with empathy and sympathy for the feelings of others. If I were to come across a homeless man digging for food in a trashcan and I had twenty dollars in my pocket, I'd buy him a meal.

However, we can all become victims of circumstance.

Brett wasn't in school on Friday; it was the day after I had my way with his shoes and the same day I overheard the conversation about Church from the two students before my mother picked me up. However, he was back on the following Monday, and I can't begin to express how satisfying seeing his broken-down face was to me. The kid looked defeated, devastated.

Of course, no one in our class knew what had really happened – except for me. But, more than the satisfaction it brought me knowing that fat little shit was completely devastated, the fact no one knew it was me made me feel incredibly empowered. Sure, it would have been amazing to have the satisfaction of Brett knowing it was me, but then I'd somehow lose my power. Secrecy was my edge, and for the first time, I felt I had a small degree of control over my life.

Something else caught my eye that morning. Brett was done, and if I ever had the motive and opportunity, perhaps I would handle him the same way again.

However, that wasn't on my mind anymore.

In class, to my right, a twinkle of light caught my eye: Erin was brushing her hair with the bedazzled hairbrush her stupid Aunt Stacey gifted her. The fact Erin had made a point of brushing her hair while standing in the middle of the class annoyed me: the girl obviously wanted to be noticed. I had to admit, it was for good reason because she was *really* pretty. Like with Brett, I couldn't figure out where sweet-looking Erin learned to be so nasty when she looked so innocent and beautiful on the outside. I learned later on in life cruel behaviors like that aren't innate, they're learned.

It's my belief that kids like Erin, Brett, all the other bullies, despite their abusive nature, truly feel how they look. They see themselves as innocent little angels because they're taught by their parents that's precisely what they are. Anything beyond their own little bubble of humanity is beyond God's reach, so they don't feel any loss of humanity or guilt when they abuse the likes of me. Shit, even I started to feel like she was angel just by looking at Erin, as much as I hated to admit it, the juxtaposition gave me clarity to understand that not all people who appear good, really are.

I didn't feel well that day. It was most likely the burger I'd eaten the night before because my parents said they felt sick that morning. Only Sarah felt fine – she'd eaten cereal for dinner. Even before class started, my stomach and bowels were rumbling loudly. Unfortunately, most of the class heard it.

I don't recall who, but someone declared, "Dude, *Pissmael* is going to shit his pants!"

I didn't respond.

Not because I didn't want to, but the combination of intense bowel pain and my own mental conditioning to hear my tormentors as barking dogs worked well together. Plus, I couldn't really pay attention – all my focus was on not *shitting* my pants.

Then I heard something I didn't want to hear during another brief moment of clarity.

"It might be because of all of that cornbread niggers eat!" It was a girl's voice. Someone responded, but I couldn't make out what was said or who said it.

The girl continued, "Yeah, his mom is black! *Eww!*" Looking up, I saw it was Erin.

I held my composure until the lunch bell rang. I sat back until all the students left the classroom. Mr. Janicek noticed and walked over to me.

"Didn't you hear the lunch bell?" he asked me, concern in his voice.

"I did. I just need a second to get up." I clutched at my aching belly for emphasis.

"Do you need to see the nurse?"

"No, it's just a cramp." I put on my bravest face. "I should be okay in just a minute."

"Okay then," my teacher said as he walked back to his desk. He gathered his things together, but just sat there. I realized he was waiting for me. It figured. There was probably some school rule that prevents students being left alone like that.

A minute later, I managed to stand up from my desk. I grabbed my books and slowly walked towards the door. Satisfied I was on my way out, Mr. Janicek stood up from his desk and left. He'd naturally assumed I would be right behind him.

Suddenly, I recalled vandalizing the Dodge bumper and Brett's Nikes – what a fucking rush they had been! Even though I wasn't entirely sure if the Dodge bumper was actually vandalized, the feeling I got from it felt as real as damaging the shoes, which I know really happened.

Once again, acting on adrenaline and pure instinct, I walked past Erin's desk, grabbed the hairbrush from her storage tray, and shoved it down the front of my pants. I quickly adjusted it so the prickly head of the brush faced my chode and the handle was behind the zipper. To the unknowing eye, I reckoned it would look like my dick. I sure as hell didn't want anyone thinking I had an inadvertent hard-on in class – like most mornings – but at least I was *supposed* to have a dick. However, I wasn't supposed to have Erin's bedazzled hairbrush resting against my balls, but the risk was definitely worth it.

That raised another question.

Worth what?

There I was, walking out of the classroom door with a fellow student's hairbrush stuffed into my pants and no idea what to do with it. The brush's handle was snug in the elastic waistband of my underpants. It would eventually slip out, but I figured I could walk a few minutes before that happened.

I made my way to the lunchroom, prickly prosthetic in place. Luckily, I had a book in my left hand – I held it in front of my crotch as I hurried in and sat down at my broken desk.

Now, I was presented with quite the dilemma: I couldn't risk being caught with the hairbrush and the gig of hiding it in my pants would likely be up the minute I stood up again. Looking around. I saw that nobody was paying me any attention. My classmates already knew I was feeling sick – they'd heard the unearthly rumblings coming from my guts and witnessed my sickly pallor. I figured maybe I could use that to my advantage…

I slumped over my desk with a loud groan to make sure a few students noticed me. Immediately, the taunts kicked off.

"Oh, man! Piss is gonna crap his pants!" someone declared. I didn't catch who, and I didn't care.

"Oh, *gross*!" another voice laughed.

"Like oh my God, he's *so* disgusting!" a female voice joined in.

It was all like music to my ears. Those stupid fucks were helping me establish my alibi. An alibi to what, I didn't know, but it was a good one nonetheless.

Upon hearing the commotion, Mrs. Allen came waddling over.

"Ishmael, if you're feeling sick, you need to go to the toilet!" she told me. I knew her choice of words was intended to get a rise out of the congregation. She wasn't British, yet she'd actually said *toilet*. Well, I hope the *bloody wanker* was satisfied because it caused my fellow students to howl with laughter.

I managed to stand up, but immediately sat back down. All eyes were on me, and the hairbrush was slipping; surely it would fall down my pant leg if I stood up! However, sitting there was no longer an option – I'd been ordered to go to the restroom. Maybe the alibi was not worth it? It seemed to be backfiring, and I still didn't know what I intended to do with Erin's hairbrush.

A solitary tear formed in my eye; I made sure nobody could see it. I wasn't crying because of the pain in my gut or the discomfort of the hairbrush stuffed in my underpants; after all, I'd brought that upon myself. It was because of what I had to do next – and I had no other choice.

As discreetly as I could, I grabbed my crotch and readjusted the hairbrush handle; the bristles were stabbing me in the balls and it didn't feel good at all. As I'd feared, some of the kids spotted my readjustment and mocked me for handling myself in public. Then, I stood up with the book held in front of my crotch and made my way out of the lunchroom and on to the restroom. As I left, I felt the colossal weight of so many eyes staring at me, judging me; I felt my inferiority as I walked towards that door.

To my left, I saw Claire sitting quietly at a table filled with sneering, laughing girls. But, as they mocked me, Claire wasn't joining in. Instead, she looked at me with empathy, sorrow, and regret – and it was all for me. Claire, *my* beautiful

Claire, didn't find me disgusting or gross – she genuinely *felt* for me, and I was falling deeper and deeper in love with her.

Once in the bathroom, I sat down in an empty stall. For the second time, I found myself locked in a bathroom stall during a time of high intensity. I really hoped it wouldn't become routine, but the outcome last time had made it so exquisite.

I finally had some time to think. Time to make a mental checklist of facts and scenarios:

1. Erin was not only a bitch, but *completely* two-faced.
2. She loved that hairbrush – the same one that was stabbing me in the testicles.
3. I had grabbed the hairbrush instinctively, without thinking.
4. I didn't know why I'd grabbed it. It's like *The Force* made me do it!
5. I couldn't be caught with the thing.
6. I'd just humiliated myself in front of the entire lunch period. Again.
7. No humiliation should go in vain.
8. I didn't have any remorse for what I did to Brett.
9. *I love Claire.*

Yeah, I was aware number nine had little to do with any of the other points, but her sorrow and sympathy had given me a revelation. I had no idea a girl could say so much with her only eyes…

However, I quickly snapped out of it – I had a hairbrush to attend to.

As I pulled it out of my pants, it scraped my ball sack. That hurt like a motherfucker.

Sitting there on the toilet, I studied Erin's hairbrush. The head appeared to be made from two pieces of plastic: I could see the seam around the edge. Bending the brush slightly, I separated the seam a little. A little further, the seam opened a tad more. Inside the gap I'd created, there were two clips holding the brush's head together. However, keeping it spread was doing a number on my fingers, and I had to let it close.

I reached into my pocket for my mechanical pencil. I bent the hairbrush again and pushed the rounded tip of the pencil right next to one of those internal clips. Once in, I used my pencil as a wrench to force the two halves apart.

There came a loud *snap*, and the hairbrush popped open on one side. With the tension lost, the other side opened immediately.

The inside of the brush was hollow, except for the rubber that held the bristles in place; I found it fascinating. Upon closer inspection, I saw how the bristles were welded together on the other side of the rubber barrier.

Even after getting so far, I still had no idea what I was doing to do with Erin's stupid brush. For a second, I wondered why I even *had* it in the first place! Then I remembered how much that nasty little girl loved insulting my mom. I recalled with anger what she'd said that morning about my mom being *black*. I wanted to introduce Erin to something that was also black.

I'm not especially proud of what transpired next, but exacting revenge is no time to worry about niceties. Looking down, I saw the toilet water below me was dirty – no doubt the result of an unsuccessful flush. So, it seemed only natural to dunk Erin's beloved hairbrush from her Aunt Stacey into the bowl. I sloshed it around to make sure to get plenty of the disgusting lavatory *chunks* inside the housing.

Erin had earned it for being so generous with her dirty mouth.

With the inside of the hairbrush well and truly contaminated, I wiped down the outside with bathroom tissue, and the outside looked just the same as before. Once satisfied, I snapped Erin's brush back together.

Unfortunately, I hadn't thought too far ahead…

In order to conceal the hairbrush again, I had to stick it back into my pants. Only, there was shit inside it, plus a thin layer on the bristles. Also, I didn't know what to do with the hairbrush; obviously, I couldn't carry it around class all day while I decided.

But, with no other choice, I stuffed it back into my pants like before. Looking at the clock mounted on the restroom wall, I saw lunch would be over in three minutes.

Talk about cutting things close.

I stepped out of the stall and walked quickly over to the door. I then made my way to the end of the hall with my book covering my crotch.

"Ishmael?" It was Mr. Decker. "What are you doing out of the lunch hall?"

"I just came out of the restroom," I told him. "There's no point going back to lunch now."

Mr. Decker nodded. "Go wait at the hallway intersection until the bell rings."

The bell rang two minutes later and I walked as fast as I could to my classroom without drawing suspicion. I had a good twenty-second lead on my classmates and I was home free.

Upon walking in, I saw Mr. Janicek sitting at his desk marking papers.

Panic gripped me: I had no idea what to do. I had to think of *something* quick before the other kids showed up. Luckily for me, Erin's desk was *en route* to my desk. As I walked by, I let the book slip from my hand.

It landed with a soft *thud*.

Mr. Janicek looked up – briefly – then looked back down. With a cast-iron excuse to be down on the floor, I knelt to pick up my book…

That's when I shoved my hands in my pants and yanked out the hairbrush. The pain as the stiff, nylon bristles ran over my balls and penis was unbearable, and I had to clench my teeth to not yell out. Unbeknownst to me at the time, I'd actually nicked and scratched my scrotum and penis.

Quickly, I slipped the hairbrush back into the storage area of Erin's desk where I'd found it and stood back up, my book in hand.

I'd completed the maneuver in just five seconds.

Not too shabby.

Soon, my classmates sauntered in. Sitting down, I feigned discomfort to keep up the façade of a bad stomach, which by then had thankfully subsided. Some scoffed and gave me the requisite dirty looks, but the intense ribbing had already died down. What the near future would hold was anybody's guess, but today I was kinda off the hook.

Part I: Chapter Ten

Curiosity must have gotten the best of my father.

Sunday morning, Sarah wasn't feeling well, so Mom decided to stay home with her. My father had heard a lot about Jadrich Lima from people at work and decided to give his *weird* sermons a try. He asked if I wanted to go along with him and, ever eager to please, I said yes. My dynamic with Dad was a strange one: despite everything – or maybe even because of it – I always relished any opportunity to receive his warm side. At the tender age of ten, the world was still small to me, so much of my self-worth and confidence came from my parents.

I didn't say much in the car; I was hoping my dad would bring something up besides school work – but that was very much the norm. I remember when I'd tried to mention Led Zeppelin or my interest in Mustangs and Camaros – he'd accused me of not having my priorities straight and lashed out with anger.

That particular Sunday, I had no interest in talking about school. I knew I wouldn't be able to express myself properly anyway: I was bullied by the other kids and looked down on by the school's staff. Talking to Dad about it would only remind me I was truly alone.

Sometimes, it felt good to just keep my dumb mouth shut.

Arriving at the Ashford Association of Patriots building, I finally saw what the renovated church had been called: *The Church of the Lima.* I was a little confused, but deduced the congregation was called the Ashford Association of Patriots and this particular chapter was called the Church of the Lima. I didn't know for sure, but that made the most sense to me.

I thought it was odd to name a church after anything other than Jesus, Mary, a saint, a holy place, or some angel or other. It was quite jarring to see it named after a mere, mortal man who likely couldn't resurrect himself after being run over by a station wagon.

I'd never seen the inside of the building before the renovations, but the new inside was truly magnificent – it was almost impossible to tell I was in a church. The walls were painted white and had wooden molding and trim. There were so many American flags I couldn't begin to count them all; on the back wall was an array of American flags from throughout history, all sporting different numbers of stars. I looked around for a confederate flag but didn't see one – it was part of American history, after all.

There weren't too many people in the Church – eight to be exact. Me and my father made it ten. We walked down the rows of polished wood pews and chose our seats near the middle. The other churchgoers saw us but refused to speak: I could tell they are avoiding us. My father appeared unphased, but I knew him well enough to know he was angry on the inside.

"This place is really cool!" I said.

"Yup," Dad agreed. "But I can't imagine how Lima paid for all of this."

I shrugged my shoulders. "So… are we going to go to this church now?"

"I don't know," my father grumbled. "I'm only here to see what's going on. We can't switch church without talking to your mother and –"

He was interrupted by a pat on his back. It was Jadrich Lima.

"Samuel! I *knew* you'd make it! Great to see you, brother!" he gushed.

"A pleasure, sir. Do you remember my son, Ishmael?" Dad said.

"Of course, I do! Thanks for coming to see us," said Lima. He seemed genuinely happy to see me, which was in stark contrast to how he'd treated me in front of the building just a few weeks prior. The only difference was it was just me and Dad – the time before, I'd had my mother and little sister with me.

"Well gentlemen, I will be starting in a few minutes." Lima looked around at his sparse congregation. "Make yourselves comfortable, and there are refreshments in the lounge." We thanked him and watched as he made his way along the pews.

"You want a drink?" my father asked me.

I nodded, but as he got to his feet, Lima stood behind the pulpit.

"Sorry, let's wait until he's done," my father whispered and sat back down.

Lima began to speak.

"I am honored and privileged to welcome you all to the Church of the Lima. I know what many of you must be thinking: who would name a church after themselves?" He let out a short, light laugh, and beamed at us all as if his church was packed out.

"I just want y'all to know the name Lima has been in my family for at least fifteen generations. The Almighty has blessed us with sons in every generation to keep the name alive. It all began so long ago that nobody in my bloodline can pinpoint exactly where it started, but please be assured the Order of the Feather dates back many, many years. I have been bestowed with the responsibility of bringing its word to the good people of Ashford."

I didn't know the fuck the *Order of the Feather* was. He said it so casually – as if it was just something we were expected to have already known.

"So… that brings me to my first sermon. I will be repeating this same sermon every Sunday for the next three weeks to make sure everyone gets the chance to hear it. I believe the people of Ashford are so very special, chosen by a higher power. I know other religions have their own interpretations of what that higher power is, but let's face it – we aren't *meant* to know. After all, have any of us actually seen Jesus? Have we seen God? Ask any Muslim if they have seen Allah or Muhammed. Have any of the mongoloids seen Buddha besides in statue form? We all know the answer, of course – we fuel belief with blind faith and nothing more. I'm not claiming to be a higher power; I am but a humble messenger. However, let's just say, *hypothetically* of course, that I was what you *might* call a God. The way to find me would not be through blind faith based upon Holy texts. It would be based upon hard evidence you can see with your own eyes. That brings me to my next point: God has never revealed himself to us directly, so what signs does He leave us to ensure we stay on the right path to Him? Signs we can see and feel? What signs has He ever left us that are not based on blind faith?

"The notion He loves us but will damn us to Hell for choosing the wrong faith is everything that is wrong with society. It gives us incentive to follow a lifestyle that may not be for the greater good. This flawed belief system is what makes us accept a reality that should be removed.

"Now, I am not here to step on anyone's toes. All I want you to do is *think*. Why would any of the good people of Ashford be destined for hell? We all know the last church held in this building made that a *real* possibility. But… why would an Almighty who loves us do such a thing?

"Look into your hearts, my brothers and sisters. Whatever higher power there exists is already righting the universe, and that is through suffering and retribution. How many of you have faced turmoil? How many of you have felt *true* pain? How many of you had to justify your lifestyle choices because some anti-American didn't believe in you?

"In the words of the great Isaac Newton, every action has an equal and opposite reaction. Now, why would God not budge on the laws of physics, but leave matters of chance and luck to be based upon faith. I for one, know the Almighty uses the same laws in all aspects of our lives. For all of our actions, the universe might be righted immediately or His plan simply won't work. He doesn't want to do that on some mysterious, catastrophic Day of Judgement. *No!* He does it right here on Earth. We face it every day, but we just don't know it.

"Now, let's be frank: Some of those other cities who preach acceptance for abhorrent people are merely sanctuaries for those who oppose the natural order of things – thus, we see the world falling into turmoil. That's why I am here, good people of Ashford. My family has traveled the world, and yet I have landed here among you. The universe sent me here because the people of Ashford are the chosen ones. We are the best representation of true Americans. Don't let the media fool you – America is a huge country and not homogenized at all. Spend a day in Kentucky and then Los Angeles – and tell me we are all the same!

"Therefore, please consider the notion our destiny is all acted out here on Earth. The day of judgement is only an ancient, Biblical metaphor, but today it doesn't work… now does it?

"We people of Ashford are united in *proper* values. We value traditional beliefs and the hard work and dedication it took to build this great country of ours. The bloodshed of history is the very life that circulates through our veins. We earned it, and the glory belongs to us!

"That ends my sermon for today. It was short, but please feel free to talk to me in the lounge. I would love to get to know each and every one of you. In congregation we stand, and with tainted blood we shall fall."

Lima finished to stunned silence from his sparse congregation.

The sermon seemed pretty vague to me, but it wasn't the first time I'd had little idea what adults were talking about. My father had a look of skepticism on his face; I mirrored his sentiments and decided Jadrich Lima was just plain confusing.

"Are we going to the lounge?" I asked my father.

Dad shook his head no. "Your mother needs help at home. Let's go."

"Can I get a drink?" I asked

"If we go back there, we'll be obliged to stay behind and talk to that man, and I don't want to right now. We have drinks at home – I'm sure you can wait five minutes." Standing up, Dad made it clear we were leaving.

Home wasn't five minutes away – it was more like twenty minutes.

Whatever.

"Ishmael, listen to me. I don't know how much the other kids talk about Lima at school, but I recommend you don't get into it. Do you hear me?"

"Yes, Dad."

"Okay, I know he seems strange, but that doesn't mean you can go around criticizing him." My father gave me a stern look. "The people in his church might not like that. Just leave it alone." His advice was good, but not realistic. If I got cornered on the subject, *not* saying anything would have my peers making up their own stories as to my loyalties to Lima.

"But what do I do if people ask me?" I ventured.

"What did I just say, Ishmael? Do you *ever* listen? Or do you just talk? Don't say anything. Don't talk about Lima. *Just leave it*," he snapped.

What started as a relatively good day with my dad suddenly went sour. Still, at least I was smart enough to hide my disdain. His advice was rarely practical, and when implementation of said advice didn't work, I'd usually get whipped, slapped, and insulted.

Ludicrous, I know, but that's the shit I had to deal with.

Part I: Chapter Eleven

When we got home, I went upstairs to find Sarah was extremely sick.

"She has a fever of 101 degrees," Mom told Dad and me as we walked into my sister's darkened bedroom.

"Ishmael! Don't go near her," Dad barked.

"Why not?" I asked, even though I knew the answer. I wanted Sarah to know the reason why I couldn't give her a cuddle.

"Because you'll catch her germs, and you have school to think about," Mom answered for him. Not sure why she had to mention school, though. So, it would be okay if I got sick during the summer? A simple *I don't want you getting sick* would have sufficed.

"Okay," I said and went to my room.

A few minutes later, when I heard my mother leave Sarah's room, I snuck back with a deck of playing cards. So, what if I got sick? I really didn't give a shit. The worse that would happen was I'd have to stay home and Mr. Janicek would send my work home. There'd be no being called Pissmael, no sitting alone at my broken desk at lunch, and no humiliation. Salvation lay within my sister's bacteria!

Actually, I thought that would make one badass death metal song: *Salvation in Bacteria.* Even better: *Salvation in Infection.*

Bullseye!

I figured I'd write the lyrics one day and send it to *Cannibal Corpse.*

"Hi, Sarah." I peeped around my sister's door.

"Hi, Iss. I'm sick." She managed a weak smile.

"I know. I brought cards. Want to play?"

"I don't know how."

"Well, can you count?" I asked her.

"Ya, I can count to twenty!"

"And you do know what the numbers look like?"

"Ya," Sarah told me with pride.

"Okay, and you know the alphabet and how the letters look?"

"Ya!" She was getting excited; she had a chance to show off her knowledge.

"Okay, then this is how you play *War*," I sat down on the edge of Sarah's bed. "I give you half of the cards, and I keep the other half. Then, we both put down the card on top. Whoever has the biggest card gets to take both cards. If you get all the cards, you win!"

Sarah looked a tad perplexed; perhaps explaining the rules was too much, given her weakened state.

"Okay, let's play." I split the deck between us.

"Now, you put down a card," I instructed.

Sarah put her top card down on the counterpane: Six of Hearts.

I put down my card: Three of Hearts.

"Okay, Duck, who has the bigger number?"

"Me!" Sarah was delighted.

"Then you win! You get to take my card!"

She took my card with glee.

A few rounds later, she put down a Queen of Hearts and I put down a Nine of Clubs.

"Umm, what I do?" said Sarah.

"All of the people cards are the biggest. The J is first, then the Q, then the K."

"I can't remember that," she huffed.

"Okay, just remember the people cards live in a castle. The prince's name is Jack. His mommy is the queen. His daddy is the king. The ace card is the highest because it's the letter A. Don't worry, we can talk about that when it happens. So, what do I have?"

"Nine!"

"Good, and what do you have?" I asked.

"Umm…"

"Remember they all live in a castle. Whose picture is that?"

"The mommy! Queen!"

"So, you win!"

Sarah took the cards with excitement.

We played a few more rounds before Sarah put down another queen. I put down a king. Once more, I explained the rules and she realized I'd won her queen. However, she was not about to go down that easily.

"Okay, its mine," I informed my little sister.

"No!" She pouted.

"Duck! Play by the rules," I said.

"Okay." She then licked the cards on both sides.

"Sarah!"

My sister gave me a cutesy look and giggled.

"Come here you!" I jumped across the bed and grabbed her. I tickled under her arms and she laughed and laughed. She even tried to tickle me back but was no match for me. Soon, she wriggled out from under me, got to the floor, and crawled away on all fours. Giving chase, I caught Sarah in my arms and held tight her for a minute; I noticed, as if for the first time, how fair my sister's skin was. Unlike me, I thought she just might make it in this world.

Part I: Chapter Twelve

The next two days in school were frustrating as hell. I hadn't seen Erin with her hairbrush and I was worried she may have taken it home and somebody had figured out something was wrong with it. Surely, she'd take it home? Given the spontaneity of what I'd done that day, I hadn't exactly thought ahead and considered all the variables.

I had not seen any indication Erin knew something was wrong: she still showed up to class as if everything was okay. I was beginning to think my spontaneous actions would produce no justice.

That soon changed.

As I sat through social studies in the afternoon, Mr. Janicek told us to work silently on an assignment until the bell rang. It was then Erin took her hairbrush out of her desk and started brushing her hair! I guess she'd left it at school after all.

I hadn't seen her use the brush since the day it made acquaintance with the toilet water. She hadn't insulted me since that day, which made the buzz of what I'd done wear off. In fact, I actually felt bad about it and thought there was a chance I'd gone too far. But feeling guilty for *her* made me feel guilty about *myself*. Had I already let myself forget her insults against me and my family?

Erin's brushstrokes were long, rhythmic, and she tilted her head to the side she brushed. She gazed off into the distance as if in some odd trance – it appeared she wasn't really focusing on anything. Erin's face was as pretty as ever, and little would anyone suspect she was so foul and profane.

I imagined the tiny particles of shit in her hair. It was the moment I'd dreamed of: I'd treated Erin how she *deserved* to be treated, but still I felt nothing. Brett's pain had been so dramatic – I'd practically *tasted* that fucker's tears as I walked by him in the hallway. As for Erin, she didn't even know the universe was conspiring against her.

But not for long.

Oh, the taste of instant gratification.

About three minutes into our silent work time, a handful of kids lifted their heads and made exaggerated sniffling noises.

"Oh man, what is that stank?" One of the boys broke the silence.

"Ahh, it *reeks*!" added another boy.

It felt good knowing I'd made an impact, but the icing on the cake was what came next. There wasn't an amount of money in the world I wouldn't have paid to see it happen…

"It stinks!" Erin gasped.

That's right, Erin! I was so happy, I actually thanked God. It took the term *holy shit* to a whole new level.

"What's going on over there?" Mr. Janicek sounded annoyed.

"Something stinks bad back here!" I chimed up.

"It must be Ishmael! Open the window!" a kid sitting near Brett shouted out. Mark started laughing from the front row, and several other students joined in.

"Enough of that!" Mr. Janicek shouted as he walked around the room, sniffing to locate the smell. He arrived at Erin's desk; my eyes were fixed on him as he looked around, as if honing in on the obnoxious whiff – I didn't want to miss one delightful minute.

Erin started to brush her hair again. Mr. Janicek focused on her, but only for a second before quickly refocusing on the A/C vent above her desk.

Oh, God almighty. Oh, the powers that be, thank you!

Mr. Janicek knew the smell was coming from Erin and that felt great to me. I suddenly forgot my fears about getting caught. What will be will be.

"I think it's the A/C vent. Please get back to work and let me call the custodian to come take a look."

We obliged, and Mr. Janicek picked up his desk phone and dialed the four numbers.

Five minutes later, Assistant Principal Brown came to our classroom. Mr. Janicek met him outside and they had a chat for a few minutes before they both came back inside.

Then, A.P. Brown addressed us: "We're having the janitor come check the A/C vent. There's nothing to worry about." He fixed his attention on Erin. "And, Miss Livingston? I have a special project in the office I'd like you to help me with. Bring your things with you."

Erin grabbed her belongings, including the hairbrush, and followed A.P. Brown with a confused look on her face. Erin was cute and popular, so no one suspected a thing. So, I decided to take matters into my own hands.

I made an audible sniffing sound and then commented semi-quietly to myself after a satisfying exhale. "Oh, man, it smells better in here now."

Only the kids sitting close by heard me, but they all looked at Erin's desk instead of me. Soon, whispers started to spread. I couldn't make out too much, but I definitely heard the words "*fart*" and "*shit herself*." The rose I'd planted in the pile of manure had finally sprouted.

I wish the story, which could be called *Erin and Aunt Stacey's Hairbrush* ended there, but it didn't. I was always a good kid at heart, but the world had not allowed me to stay that way: I'd been pushed too far. Erin was going to feel how Brett had; I'd ruined her reputation, but I still felt the need to ruin something far worse – her confidence.

And I knew exactly how to do it.

Once class was over, I stayed behind just a few minutes scrutinizing my social studies book, but that was just a ruse.

"Staying behind again, Ishmael?" Mr. Janicek asked me.

"Not long. Should I go?" I asked him.

"No, but I need the restroom. Can I trust you be here by yourself?"

"Yeah, I'll just be at my desk."

My teacher got up and left.

I had my chance: Walking over to Mark's desk, I removed a sheet of notebook paper from his pack, and then took a purple pen from his gel pen set – he often showed off about his fancy pens and even did some in-class assignments with them. That pretentious little prick would soon learn the consequences of showboating.

I slipped the pen in my pocket and walked back to my desk in the corner. I used the paper from Mark's desk because I thought using my own paper could be used to give me away – I'd seen enough TV shows where they shade a sheet of paper with a pencil to reveal the culprit's writing to know not to risk it. With Mark's purple pen, I wrote "you smell like shit" on the paper. And, being left-handed, I used my right to disguise my handwriting. Once done, I folded the paper up three times and tucked it into my pocket. I swiftly returned to Mark's desk and slipped the gel pen back into the case.

I thought Mr. Janicek was still in the restroom, so I decided it was a good time to leave. I picked up my backpack and headed towards the door… just as Mr. Janicek walked back in.

"Leaving?" he asked.

"Yeah, I need to get home."

"Okay, but we talked about this," Mr. Janicek said sternly. "If you stay behind, you can't just leave unless you tell me. Do you understand, Ishmael?"

"I'm sorry." I nodded. Of course, he had no idea what I'd just done, but that didn't stop me feeling nervous.

"Okay then."

I was almost out the door when he called after me. "Hey, Ishmael?"

I spun around. "Yes?"

"How about tomorrow you take your original desk back – the one next to Mark? It is *your* desk after all." He smiled at me.

"It's okay. I like where I sit now," I told him.

"Are you sure?" My teacher looked perplexed, but sounded *caring* towards me, which I sadly found to be very odd.

"Thanks, Mr. Janicek, but can I stay where I am?"

He looked at me with a somber expression. "Of course, you can."

"Okay. See you tomorrow," I said as I left the classroom.

Turning the corner into the hallway, I went to Erin's locker…

Except, I couldn't remember exactly *which* locker was hers. I could only narrow it down to one of three possible. It was shit-or-bust time: I had to make up my mind. I had a one third chance of getting it right, and I knew I had to hedge my bets of the message getting to Erin. So, thinking fast, I pulled a pen out of my pocket, along with the note, and used my right hand to scrawl *Erin* on the back. Then, if I did put it into the wrong locker, it would no doubt be passed on.

Done, I folded up the note and slipped it through the vents in the middle locker.

I knew Erin would see the message and never know who'd written it, though a part of me was hoping she would suspect Mark. She'd also know the class believed it was her who had made the shitty smell; her confidence and self-worth would vanish as fast as she'd made mine each time she insulted me and my mother.

I walked over towards the front of the school to exit at the front. Passing the nurse's office, I heard crying inside; it was Erin. I couldn't be sure if the girl was embarrassed or the situation had gotten too much for her, but it sure felt good to hear her cry.

Bitch.

Part I: Chapter Thirteen

For the next three days, Erin didn't show up to school. It felt good for me to have the attention of my classmates shift to someone else. They had a new punching bag, and it was nice to know I'd caused it.

That Saturday, my father had a work party to attend and there was only space for one guest. Sarah was still getting over her illness and needed taking care of, so my father took me along instead of my mother.

And so, for the second time in that month, I was alone with my dad on an outing. It was odd, but I didn't fear him quite as much when we were alone. Not that he wasn't a bully when it was just the two of us, but he seemed to show me a tad more respect than he did at home.

I really couldn't explain it.

The work party was over forty-five minutes away. Dad talked to me as he drove. In an effort to not ruin our time together, I was mindful to speak only when spoken to.

"I know you can see how many motherfuckers are in the world," Dad said. "So many uneducated pieces of shit out to make life miserable for others. Your books are your ticket out, the way to a higher place."

"How so?" I asked.

"Do you *ever* think about such things, Son? Or do you only think about watching your stupid TV shows?" I don't think my father caught the irony in his words. "When you do well in school, you get into a good college. From there, you can get a good job that pays well. That means you can live in a better area."

I found it funny that he was describing himself, but we'd ended up in Ashford, Ohio.

I knew there had to be more to the endeavor than simply the pursuit of academic prowess; perhaps certain soft skills were in order, but it would be many years before I realized how unequipped I was to live in the real world.

"I get bullied a lot at school," I told him. "I try to get my work done, but it's hard."

"I thought I told you to ignore them," Dad said, and I knew better than to press him on the matter.

"Yeah," I agreed and closed my mouth.

***

We arrived at the event hall and went inside. While I walked alongside my dad, I was behind him in spirit. I really had no idea how to act in such formal situations.

Inside, we were immediately were greeted by a gentleman who appeared middle-aged but younger than Dad.

"Well, look who it is! How are you, Greg?" Dad exclaimed as if the guy was a long-lost friend.

"Samuel! Great to see you! Hope the drive was okay."

"Didn't even notice it."

"Sorry about your daughter," Greg said. "I'd have loved to see your lovely wife again. I thought you were bringing your son with you?"

"This is my son." Dad pushed me forward a little. "Greg, meet Ishmael. Ishmael, meet Mr. Greg. Now what do you say, Son?"

"Nice to meet you, Mr. Greg," I offered. Of course, I didn't know the man's last name, so I attempted to

to be respectfully witty. It seemed to work.

"Ha ha! That's my boy!" Dad gave me a hearty clap on the shoulder.

"And quite the smart one, at that." Greg smiled at me. "But Ishmael, please call me Greg."

"I don't think I am allowed, sir. Can you know your last name?"

"A young man of manners *and* respect." Greg was impressed. "You have taught him well, Sam! Well then, Ishmael, I think *Mr. Greg* will do just fine. I shall save you a seat right next to me and my wife. Get yourself over to the snack table and grab something to eat – and all the sodas you want, Son."

"Thank you, Mr. Greg," I said and wandered off.

I'd never seen such an elaborate snack table in my whole life. Each individual piece of cubed fruit looked handcrafted and had its own mini plastic sword in it for easy consumption. Grabbing a small plate, I loaded up on mini chicken sliders, strawberries, and a bottle of Pepsi. I noticed the cap was on the bottle, but before I could even look around to see how to remedy the situation, a man who looked like a butler approached and popped the cap off with a silver bottle opener. He wore white gloves and black bowtie and looked incredibly smart.

He was black, and quite likely the first black person other than Mom I'd seen since moving to Ashford.

I had no idea where Dad and Mr. Greg were sitting, and it proved to be quite the challenge to find them while balancing two mini plates and an open bottle of Pepsi. I'd walked about ten feet away from the snack table before the butler gentlemen approached, took the bottle and plates from me, and helped me find my table.

Once I'd done so, the nice gentlemen walked with me to the table. There, he placed the plates and drink down and pulled out my chair.

"Ishmael, did you ask this gentleman to carry your things?" my father asked, his tone already condemning me.

"Sir, the young gentleman asked for no such thing," the butler gentleman replied. "It was my choice to help him, and I wouldn't hear no for an answer. Your son is very well-mannered."

"Well, okay then." Dad seemed placated by the answer. "Ishmael, what do you say?"

"Thank you for your help, sir," I said.

The gentleman placed his hand over his heart, bowed his head, and walked quietly away.

I was pissed off like a motherfucker at that point, but I held my peace as always. It was routine for me to be constantly criticized by my mother and father for being a child of no manners. However, I was never actually given the goddamn chance. Rather than having me grow up to be young a man of manners and refinement, it was more important for my parents to be the ones being seen as having such high standards. Had I been the one to say *thank you* to the nice butler gentleman without being prompted, it would have attributed my good manners to *me*. And that would rob my dad of the honor of being seen as a parent who *demands* his son show respect.

It was more about him than me; I'm surprised he didn't remind me to wipe the shit from my ass when I excused myself to go to the restroom.

No time for that, though. Those battered chicken sliders had my name all over them. One bite, and I quickly forgot about what had irked me. Damn, they were good!

"So, Sam, are you still attending Melinda's for Sunday service?" asked Mr. Greg.

"I am, but not last Sunday," said Dad.

"That's why I asked. I wasn't there either."

"No?" Dad sounded surprised.

"I actually went to that new church," Mr. Greg said. "I saw you and Ishmael there."

"Oh really? I'm sorry, I didn't notice you. What do you think about Jadrich Lima?"

"Truth is, I can't tell if that's even a *church*," Mr. Greg replied. "He didn't mention anything about the Bible at all, and I saw no crosses or any references to Christianity. Not sure why he calls it a church."

"I wondered about that, too," said Dad.

"I'll tell you something, Sam. Some things Lima said *did* make sense. Now, I wasn't a fan of him outright rejecting our faith as we practice it, but he certainly recognized the things ruining our country."

"Will you be going back, Greg?"

"I don't know how I can make time for Melinda's service *and* Lima, but for the time being, I'm going to see what he's all about and what he has to do with those that threaten our way of life." Then Mr. Greg's attention turned to me.

"How you liking them sliders, Son?" he asked.

"They're the best I've *ever* had!"

"Well, alright then. I was just telling your daddy I saw you both at the new church last weekend. How did *you* like that Lima fellow?"

"I didn't really understand what he was talking about, but I thought he was really nice."

Just then, a young black woman came to our table. She was dressed smart like the butler gentleman and spoke eloquently to my dad. "Sir, will the young gentleman be enjoying the adult entrée, or shall we provide a children's menu?"

"Tell her if you want the kid's menu or the adult meal, Ishmael," Dad ordered me. "Can you finish a whole adult dinner?" With me being the only kid at the clearly adult function, I was surprised they even had a kid's menu.

"We will happily box up any leftovers," said the young lady.

"Well, okay, then you can share some with your sister," Dad said. "Tell her you want the adult menu. Tell her *right now*." The server awaited my response; it was comforting to know the situation was as awkward for her as it was for me.

"I'll have the adult menu, please."

"Very good, sir." The young lady walked away.

Once she was out of earshot, my father leaned towards me and spoke softly. "Have some manners the next time you come to this kind of event. I shouldn't have had to tell you to answer her question!"

With no appropriate response, I turned back to my chicken sliders and strawberries. Sadly, the food didn't look as appetizing, but I ate it all anyway to avoid my father's displeasure at not clearing my plate. There was something about eating after being humiliated that added a new layer of degradation. Thinking back, it was highly inappropriate for him to take me to a function consisting of adults and their spouses in the first place. I don't know what he was thinking.

"So, what about Lima interested you?" Dad picked up with Mr. Greg.

"Look, Sam, you're a smart man, so I can tell you straight," Mr. Greg said with a wise smile. "Our way of life is constantly being shit on by fools who talk about having an open mind. Except, that *open mind* is always about crazy things – like a man laying with a man, and so forth. When we call bullshit, we're told we need to open our eyes. Don't you see, Sam?"

"What about Lima's rhetoric about Ashford folks being the chosen ones?"

"I don't know, Sam, I really don't." Mr. Greg shook his head and frowned. "But what I *do* know is people have the ability to make a choice. However, a *bad* choice leads to bad ideas being spread to their children, and a few generations later, the collective thought process is all wrong. Maybe it's not their fault, but breeding can make some people more susceptible to believing in the *wrong* things. Just look at all those crazy Muslims out there. Now, I know they believe in what they were born into, and it's not entirely their fault, but that won't soothe the eventual burn, now will it?"

"I guess not," agreed Dad.

"So, I think that's what Lima meant by chosen ones." Mr. Greg seemed pleased with his explanation, although it didn't make much sense to me at all. "How about this, Sam. I understand Lima's actual teachings will start next week. I say, just this week, let's go together and see what the man's *really* all about."

"Sure, I'll be there." Dad nodded.

"If you'll excuse me, gentlemen, I'll be right back. Nature calls." Mr. Greg upped and headed off to restroom.

"Dad, I though you said you didn't like that Lima guy," I said.

"I don't," my father snapped back. "But you keep your mouth shut when Greg comes back. Not a damn word out of you, or you'll get it at home. Understand? If he asks, say you *are* interested – and make it sound *positive*!"

"But…" I began before being interrupted by the most threatening face I'd ever seen in my life. "Okay…"

A few moments later, Mr. Greg returned to the table, followed by a bunch of servers carrying salmon with lemon sauce with a side of mashed potatoes and mixed vegetables. The presentation looked to be even better than the food itself, but after just one bite, it was evident the food carried its own weight.

"You know, I'm often disappointed when I come back to find my food waiting for me," Mr. Greg told the table.

"Why is that?" Dad asked. "Most people enjoy that."

"I guess being served is part of my experience, ya know? It's nice to be on the receiving end of formality. The other side is something I might never understand."

"Not understand, Greg?" My father seemed puzzled.

"Come on, now. Men like us aren't meant to serve. That role is for... *others*. And, don't get me wrong, I'm sure they enjoy it; there is great pride to be had in showing respect and doing it well."

My dad looked pissed off.

Surely Mr. Greg knew my mother was black, and I was more on the black side of appearance than the white side, but Mr. Greg spit his bigotry anyway. I didn't know what his point was, but I felt awful seeing my Dad feel so bad. He was the man I feared more than anyone and one of my main sources of pain, but I suppose I found sympathy for the tyrant reduced to such raw human emotion.

However, Dad didn't have much time to wallow in his aggrievance: a man and woman from the hospitality desk were walking around, discretely asking people something. I saw a few guests look over towards my father and point at him.

Soon, the man and woman were at our table. "Sir, would you be Mr. Abias?" asked the woman.

"I am."

"Sir, you have a very important call at the front desk. Your car has already been valeted to the front of the hotel."

"Is something the matter?" Dad's face was suddenly the picture of concern.

"I believe so, sir. The call is from your wife. She's at the hospital."

"Ishmael, we need to go," Dad barked at me. "Ma'am, where can I take the call?" Everyone in the hall was looking our way.

"Right this way, sir," said the man, and he rushed us to the lobby where the receptionist waited with the phone in her hand. My dad answered; I only heard his end of the call.

"Hello...Yes, I'm here, and he is too...What's going on?... Why...You mean Ishmael?... Okay, hold on..."

He desperately looked at the receptionist. "Ma'am, my wife needs my son in on this call as well. I'm not sure why."

"Of course. Young man, come with me, please." She gave me a reassuring smile and led me to another phone just a few feet away. She pressed a few buttons and the phones connected.

"I'm here," said Dad.

"And Ishmael?" asked Mom

"I'm here, too, Mom," I said.

"I'm at the hospital with Sarah. Her fever reached 106 degrees, and she might not survive. I need you both here as soon as you can." Mom choked on the tears I knew she was holding back. "I'm putting Sarah on the phone now. Say anything you need to say… you know… just in case."

"What?" Dad screamed into the phone.

"I'm giving her the phone," Mom said through a muffled cry.

"No, don't do that! Don't talk like that!" Dad cried, but it was too late and Sarah was on the line.

"Hi, Daddy." Sarah sounded *really* sick.

"Sweetheart, don't you worry, I'm on my way, and nothing will happen to you. Just hang on for me and your brother, okay?"

"Okay, Daddy. Where did Iss go?"

"I'm here," I said, "I love you, Monkey. I love you so much. You're going to be okay, but just in case –"

"ISHMAEL!" Dad cut me off. "Don't 'just in case' like a madman. Nothing will happen. We need to go – now!" Dads grabbed my hand.

Sarah said something, but I had no idea what.

Granted, I also wanted to believe Sarah would be just fine. But what if she wasn't? I'd have loved to hear what she'd said next…

The valets had our car waiting with the engine running, and in a few seconds, we were driving away.

Part I: Chapter Fourteen

D ad and I didn't speak a single word in the car. The road was dark, foreboding, and my father shook as he drove.

Soon, we reached the two-lane freeway between the hotel and our part of Ashford; it had no discernable features, other than the intermittent yellow dashes and the occasional tree at its side.

At that moment, I realized just how insignificant I really was. I thought about the kids at school who bullied me without remorse. I thought about how their self-perception of Godliness was untouched by their treatment of me, thanks to their birthright. It made me wonder if they were to blame, or was it the parents who influenced them?

We got to where the highway had no streetlights – it was amazing to think that our car was enveloped in darkness; all we could see was the 200 or so feet ahead lit up by the headlights. I wondered how the moon would see us – if it could see. Perhaps just a dark area of land in Ashford Ohio? And, within that darkness, a small bubble of light moving with urgency along a lightless road. At that moment in time, the entirety of my existence was in that bubble. My pain, pent up aggression, fears, life experiences, and physical dominion were all contained in that miniscule bubble of light.

There were two people within, living everyone's worst nightmare, and yet the emotion of the situation was contained within that single point of light, which was so insignificant compared to the rest of the world upon which the moon looked down. The moon would also see New York City, Los Angeles, Houston, large bodies of water, or perhaps a tornado in Kansas. Other times, it would see the Demilitarized Zone between the two Koreas and the difference in light between East and West Berlin, remnants of a time gone wrong.

Next to all that, the little point of light driving down the road in Ashford was surely insignificant. Yet, within it, a man and his son had just possibly said their last words to their daughter and sister...

In that tiny speck of light, the rest of the universe was what was truly insignificant.

Part I: Chapter Fifteen

M y father and I ran into the hospital with no regard as to whether we were supposed to park where we did; it's astounding that hospitals actually have rules as to when and where one can park, and often charges extortionate fees during times of deep distress. Nobody goes to a hospital for the cafeteria.

We ran up to the receptionist, completely out of breath. "Sarah Abias… please," Dad panted.

"Please spell the name."

"S-A-R-A-H A-B-I-A-S." I could tell Dad was fighting to maintain some composure.

"Floor Nineteen, room Six-B. The elevator is down the hall to your left, on the right-hand side."

"Thanks," Dad said with a strained smile. "Ishmael, come on."

We ran down the hallway as fast as we could and made our way to the nineteenth floor. There, we heard Mom's voice yelling all the way down the hall.

"Mom!" I cried out as Dad and I arrived at six-B. She ran toward us and embraced us both together.

"Is she okay?" I asked.

"Ishmael, not now! Madilyn, is she doing okay?" asked Dad.

"She seems to be for now, but they need to keep her here overnight," Mom told him. "She had an ear infection that got out of hand. After I called you, her temperature came down to 101 degrees. Hopefully they'll get it back to normal."

"Can we see her?" I asked.

"Yes, we can all go in." Mom gave me a reassuring smile.

"No talking when we go inside the –" Dad said.

"Sam, cool it," Mom interrupted. "Please, cool it, okay? Ishmael can say what he wants to his sister."

The three of us walked in to see Sarah laying in the hospital bed covered in wires and tubes. She was awake but not very mobile. Her gaze turned towards me.

"Hey, Monkey!" I greeted her with the biggest grin I could muster.

Sarah smiled at me and looked as if she wanted to say something. I knew it would take a lot of effort, so I gestured her to stay quiet. "It's okay, Monkey, you don't have to say anything. Everything is gonna be just fine. You're just a little sick, that's all."

End of Part One

January

Huntsville Texas

"I'm intrigued," said Dr. Russell. His words were few; Ishmael knew he was genuine.

"I'm glad," replied Ishmael.

Dr. Russell stood up and paced a few steps back and forth. He remained within the vicinity of the table. It made Ishmael nervous.

"What are you thinking about? Pondering the origins of this crazy nigger in prison?"

"No, Ishmael. I don't think this way, and I am certain you know that."

"Then *what*?"

With a deep breath, the doctor continued. "Let's face it, Ishmael. You *belong* behind these walls. Please forgive my bluntness. However, I am plagued regularly by patients who aren't smart enough to understand how they wrote their own fate. That's why it's refreshing to speak to you. You have the ability to understand, and the truth is that you really do belong in here."

Ishmael, despite being a fellow Harvard graduate, could not figure out the shrink's angle. It confused him. "That's what you wanted to tell me?" he said. He gripped his bandaged hand with his other; it felt as if the stiches may have worked loose. He didn't wish to make it obvious though, so he feigned not feeling anything.

Dr. Russell sat back down in his chair, clasped his hands, and looked directly at Ishmael.

"There is a point. Society will label you as a criminal. Sure, you do have quite a few supporters, but you must realize they don't think you're innocent. They simply support your crime. You are defined by your infamy. But I might be one of the few people who sees you as a person. As something other than just a criminal with notoriety."

Ishmael sat back in the uncomfortable chair.

"Tell me more about Claire," Dr. Russell asked bluntly.

"Huh?"

"Did you manage to keep in touch with her after you left Ashford?"

Ishmael was lost for words and had trouble getting them out. "Wh-wh-what?"

"Why so confused, Ishmael? You mentioned her many times. Besides your little sister, she must have been your only warmth in such a cold place," Dr. Russell explained.

"I guess you could say that," Ishmael grumbled. "That school was where souls went to die and demons are born. I still don't know how she ended up there."

"Are you still upset at your parents?"

"Doctor, you're throwing really deep questions at me – one after the other. Like, what the fuck? Just chill out and…"

"Answer my question. Do you still harbor anger towards them?"

"Yeah, but its better I continue not speaking to them. They weren't with me when I went to Harvard and they don't visit me here. Not after what my dad insinuated…" Ishmael suddenly stopped speaking.

"No, no, Ishmael. Please go on. Tell me about Sarah. I know about the trauma you suffered because of her, but all I have to go on are police reports, news reports, and word of mouth. And, sadly, some religious interpretation."

"How can you say that shit to me? *Officer Mistry!*"

"Please, Ishmael. Do you think I subscribe to their thinking?"

"Officer Mistry! *Motherfucker!* Let's ride." Ishmael signaled he was finished.

Dr. Russell looked directly into Ishmael's eyes with a soft expression – as if hoping to wear him down. He knew Ishmael didn't really wish to leave. He was only making a statement. He kept his gaze on Ishmael even as Officer Mistry approached, knelt down by the chair, and started removing the shackles.

"Ishmael, look at the men behind those walls," Dr. Russell urged. "If not with me, the only ears to be offered to you are from murderers and pederasts. You might not admit it now, but you will miss me."

Officer Mistry snapped the ankle shackles back into place and stood Ishmael up. Ishmael refused to look at the doctor.

"Okay, Ishmael. When you are ready to see me again, I'll be here. Remember that, Ishmael. I will be here to hear the *real* Ishmael Abias. And, by the way, I don't think your stitches burst. Just try not to twist your hand like that, and everything should be fine.

Ishmael took a deep breath and shook his head to the officer, signaling he wants to stay for just another second.

"What do you want to know?

"I want to know more about the incident with your sister." The doctor looked relieved. "No notes. Just my ear. Tell me *everything*. Afterwards, you decide if I can help you or if you want me gone. As for now, I will take my leave."

Signaling towards the door, Officer Mistry took Ishmael back into the general prison population.

***

It was another three weeks before Ishmael called Dr. Russell back to the prison. During the time in between, Ishmael spent the entire time in solitary confinement after an incident where he beat a *chomo* to near death during lunch. The child molester had been telling people he was in prison for a robbery, but the true nature of why he was there had soon spread through the prison and Ishmael had decided to take the law into his own hands. Vigilante justice.

Part II

The Tears of Sarah

Part II: Chapter One

"Mr. Abias, we're giving Sarah IV antibiotics to lower her temperature," the beautiful, olive-skinned nurse told my father. "The doctor will be in to see you in a just a few minutes."

"Thank you…umm…I didn't catch your name," my father said.

"Nurse Middleton. Just call me Emily." The nurse nodded down to the name badge resting on the curve of her breast.

"Thank you."

"If you need refreshments, there are vending machines in the lounge down the hall."

Mom sat quietly on the couch in the waiting room; Sarah was resting and Nurse Middleton had suggested we all step out of her room. My poor mother had cried so much, she could cry no further; she simply sat there staring off into the distance.

"Mom, can I go see Sarah again?" I asked.

"She's asleep, Ishmael," she told me, her voice flat.

"Yeah, but I need to see if she's okay."

"Your mother said –" my father butted in.

"Sam, please! Okay, Ishmael, let's go." Mom led me to my sister's room.

I suppose any little girl would look vulnerable swamped by a hospital bed with tubes and wires snaking out of her, but Sarah looked so helpless and frail laying there – she looked like a victim. Granted, her aggressor was not some vicious criminal, but I still felt but feel the injustice done to my sister stemmed from some malice as opposed to sheer bad luck.

Sarah's eyes were closed but she didn't look like she was asleep. To me, it looked like she was in prison, held against her will, and I couldn't help her because the prison's walls were her own body. I began feeling angry, but it quickly subsided when Sarah opened her eyes and turned her head toward me.

"Iss?" Sarah's voice was gentle, raspy.

"Hi, Monkey!" I said.

"I still sick."

"I know, Monkey, but you'll be home soon. Okay? It's not so bad here." I smiled.

"Okay. Play card games?"

"Of course!" I promised.

"Okay, bye," she whispered as she fell back to her much-needed sleep.

My mother looked at me. She cared for us both deeply, even though I was usually on the receiving end of her pent-up frustration and anger. However, for a moment, I actually *felt* my mother's love.

"What's going on, Mom?" I asked her, confused by the alien feelings she stirred within me.

"Your sister never accepted anything was going to be alright until you told her so," she explained.

Not knowing what to say, I simply shrugged my shoulders and followed my mother back to the waiting room.

My father was waiting for us. He stood up as we walked in. "So, did you wake her up?" he demanded.

"No," I lied.

"Good, because if you did, I'll be very angry."

Mom decided she'd be the one to spend the night in the hospital with Sarah – *just in case*. Dad also wanted to, but they both felt staying there would be too stressful on me, so they planned alternate nights, should that be necessary. Believe me, I wanted to spend the night by my little sister's side, and I had the physical and mental strength to do so – but, of course, my parents knew better.

As my father drove me home, I thought about what my mother had said on the phone: just what the hell had she meant about it potentially being the last time I'd see Sarah? Sure, she'd made it clear it was only a *possibility*, but it still felt harsh. I knew death was real, but I never believed it would happen to *us*. Such tragedies were reserved for other families.

"Hey Dad?"

"Yes?"

"Why did Mom on the phone say this might be the last time we saw Sarah?"

"She's upset and Sarah is sick. I guess your mother got a little emotional," he said, clearly irritated.

"But, why would she even *think* that?" I pressed him against my better judgement.

"Your sister had a fever high enough to kill someone her age," Dad told me. "But that's what hospitals are for."

"I know, but Mom said –"

"Don't worry about what your mom said," Dad raised his voice. "That was then, and this is now. Sarah will be perfectly fine, so less of your morbid talk."

"I know, but I was just thinking about it –"

"You know, I've never known a kid more morbid than you, Ishmael. *Just shut up!*" he screamed, his face red with anger.

Even faced with the prospect of losing my sister – his daughter – I couldn't have a man-to-man conversation with my father. He didn't care about my heart or my feelings, and he obviously never considered I'd just been told I might not see my sister again, nor the deep psychological implications of hearing such a thing. My family had never faced such a crisis before, but I'd always had faith we'd pull together if it ever did.

All of my faith disappeared that night.

***

Next morning, just as I awoke from a fitful night's sleep, I heard Dad talking to my mother on the phone.

"*You told his school?* What difference does it make? Nothing is stopping Ishmael from his work. Yes… Yes, I know…"

I *had* to know what they were talking about.

What was the worst they could do if they caught me eavesdropping? Dad would likely beat me, and my mom would scream how much she wished she'd never had me.

Meh. I got used to that shit.

I always used to think my life couldn't get worse, but seeing my sister – the only pure thing in my world – in a hospital bed with a very real prospect of dying had made me realize things could be *so* much worse.

I crept into my parent's bedroom. Dad wouldn't question why I was going in because my books and study materials were stored there as my room was pretty small.

Leaving the door open, I looked around; I needed something that would make a sound but not break easily.

A textbook.

Brilliant!

I carried my Social Studies book to the en suite bathroom and dropped it flat on the tiles. The noise resounded throughout the entire house. It *had* to have caught my father's attention downstairs.

Now I wasn't sure if he would react, but couldn't afford the time to find out: I ran over to his bedside phone and took it off the hook.

"Hey! What happened?" Dad called from downstairs.

"Just dropped my book!" I yelled back as I gripped the phone receiver with the palm of my hand as hard as I could.

"Be careful, *please*!" The exasperation in his voice was clear.

Dad returned to his phone call; much to my relief neither he nor my mom seemed to notice the slight change in background noise.

"Sam, you know and I know he's facing things you can't understand," I heard my mom say.

"What are you talking about? He's my son. Of course, I know."

"Yes, *your* son, but Ishmael is *black* like me. Your way of having him study hard may help him make money one day, but it's not helping his mental state right now. Those filthy redneck bullies at school are cruel, but they're going to have some sympathy for Ishmael with his sister being in the ER. If you care so much about our son's future, Sam, quit being a military general and be a real father for once."

"Madilyn!" Dad snapped. "Are you crazy? My discipline, at the very least, will ensure a good future for Ishmael. I can't imagine what you'll tell him when he misses the chance to get into a good university, but at least his *feelings* weren't hurt." My father's voice was loud enough for me to hear without listening in on the phone.

"His feelings *matter*!" Mom raised her voice to him – something she rarely did.

"Yeah? I'll remember that the next time you get upset and tell him he should have never been born."

At that moment, it was hard to decide which devil to dance with.

"Fine, Sam, fine. I deserved that. I've made the decision: the school knows what's happened, and you'll just have to accept it! His lunch is in the oven. Set the timer to twenty minutes on 350."

"Wait –"

"I have nothing more to say to you, Sam."

"Fine, don't talk to me. But it's about lunch. I'm taking Ishmael to Lima's church."

"Pardon me?"

"I know, *Middy*, but listen. My job is as important as Sarah's treatment. If I lose my health insurance, we'll be sent to a charity hospital – and I can't risk that."

"I don't believe you."

"This is no time for your ridiculous ideals!" My father's retort was curt. "You always said you'd take to the streets if you had to for our children, so why can't I have the privilege of selling out my religious principles? You act as if I *want* to see that Lima *sonnofabitch*! I'll just go, shake some hands, make sure I'm seen by people from my work, and then leave. That's *all*!"

"Do whatever you think is best, Sam." Mom sounded weary. "Sarah has been without me long enough because of you. Goodbye."

She hung up.

I heard Dad say a sad *bye* into the dead phone line; it was not often I saw that vulnerability in him.

Odd though, they'd never spoken about Sarah's condition on the phone. I figured it wouldn't be something they'd pass on, no matter how much animosity there was between them. They must have discussed that before I'd woken up.

Soon, I heard footsteps coming up the stairs. I quickly returned the phone to its cradle on Dad's nightstand and headed to the restroom. I picked up my Social Studies book along the way, placing it next to the sink. Seconds later, I came out to find my father leafing through some work documents.

"Looks like it's just you and me this weekend," he growled.

"Yeah."

"Well, I've got a surprise for you – we're going to the Ashford Association of Patriots for lunch and Lima's sermon."

Naturally, I couldn't act *too* surprised, nor could I give away that I already knew.

"Are you sure, Dad? You said you didn't like that man."

"I know," my dad sighed. "I'll explain later."

"Is it because we can pray for Sarah?"

"If you want to do that, you can,"

I was pretty fucking shocked by that response.

Church wasn't for three more hours, so Dad told me to fix myself something to eat and watch TV until he called me.

It may have been a Sunday, but the selection of cartoons was plentiful. So, I sat down in front of the television and enjoyed myself. In the back of my mind, though, I couldn't get my mind off my sister – it still felt good to escape into the Looney Tunes.

And, for a moment or two, I had no honor to protect, no locker combinations to steal, no shoes to destroy, no hairbrushes to hide fecal matter in. All that shit was where it belonged.

I must have watched several whole cartoons without as much as blinking. As always, wisecracking Bugs Bunny outsmarted *everyone*, and I couldn't stop laughing.

Part II: Chapter Two

A few hours later, we arrived at the church – a little late. We didn't have time to socialize as Lima was just taking to the pulpit as we walked in. We could have sat at the back and not attracted attention, but Dad wanted to make sure he was seen. So, he sat us in the pew with two spare seats in the middle near the aisle.

"Now this…" Lima began. "This right here warms my heart and confirms my predilection for the good people of Ashford. Before, we were but a few, but I now see us growing in numbers. Indeed, you are nothing less than The Chosen!

"For those joining us for the first time today, I'm Jadrich Lima, your new preacher here at the Ashford Association of Patriots! My first three sermons were all identical – an introduction to myself. If you missed them, I have recorded copies for sale. However, today is the day I deliver my first *real* sermon. Now, give me a show of hands, how many of you today follow the word of God's only son, none other than Jesus Christ Himself?"

A sea of hands went up.

"I'm not surprised at all by this – I wouldn't expect anything less from those who are inspired. After all, He died for our sins, and only through Him shall we see salvation! Now, why do you think we see such calamity and disaster all over the world? Well, maybe, just *maybe* if mankind stopped making up deities based on Pagan rituals, they might bask in the light! But sadly, that won't happen.

"Let's start with the Jews, as an example. Intellectual, oh yes, indeed! But *strong*? How can that be? Well, ask Pharoah and Hitler, and there you have a people that cannot fend for themselves. Even today, in their homeland, they only survive with the protection of those who believe they have Christ on their side. Now let's move on to the Hindus of India. Some see their country as a mystical nation of everlasting beauty and inspiration... but you couldn't pay me enough to take a bath in that sacred river that's not fit for a rest-stop toilet. I don't know about y'all, but if I were to pray directly to a statue, I wouldn't exactly expect it to pray back – unless I was crazy! And, of course, I save the best for last. The Religion of Peace! None other than Islam! Muslims... they cause trouble everywhere they go and never let *anyone* live in peace! Just ask the Hindus in India, Jews in Israel, and the Christians in Europe and the United States who live among them. Violence, war, and anger is all Muslims bring to the table. Every non-Muslim country they live in, they ask the indigenous population to conform to *their* belief system. No respect at all.

"The refusal to accept the true Messiah is the reason all those people went astray, and it is acceptance in the Messiah that will bring them back. Therefore, today's lesson is that we should see those *people* for what they really are; only their resistance to the good. Yet anybody can be saved, and we must do all we can to help others see the light."

Lima talked for at least thirty more minutes; I zoned in and out after a short while – it all sounded like nonsense to me. Soon, the congregation stood up, and I knew Lima's bullshit was finally over.

"Can we go now, Dad?" I asked.

"We're having lunch here, remember?"

"But –"

"Samuel," Greg interrupted me. "I'm *so* sorry to hear about little Sarah. I hope you don't mind, but I spoke to your wife this morning."

"Yes, she told me you called. Thank you for your concern." Dad smiled.

"So… is everything alright? I may ask how come you're here this morning?"

"I'm heading back to the hospital after this." Dad seemed eager to offer some explanation to the man. "But I needed faith and blessings to keep my mind fresh. Same for Ishmael."

"Young man, your sister is always in my prayers," Greg addressed me with a serious tone. "Keep strong, and know the closer your knees are to the floor, the closer your heart is to God." It struck me as personal, intimate advice to give to someone else's kid, and I had to stand there like a little bitch and thank him for telling me how to cope. I didn't want to hear that from him.

"Thank you, sir, I'll pray," I told him solemnly.

"Look, Sam, don't worry about coming into the office. Seriously… it's perfectly okay, given the circumstances," said Greg.

"No, no, Greg, I can come in. I need to focus on other things or I'll be no good to Sarah. It's all fine, boss."

"Well, if I can't convince you, just let me know if you need anything." Greg fixed Dad with a thin smile. "So, what did you bring for the lunch pot luck?"

"What was that?"

"Aren't you having lunch with us?"

"Yes, but…"

"The bulletin board around town said all lunch participants are to bring a dish," Greg told my father. "You have too much on your plate right now, I'm sure Lima will understand...

"No... no..." Dad was visibly embarrassed. "We have to head back to the hospital."

"Okay, Sam. See you at the office tomorrow."

We made our way back to the car. While driving, my father didn't say a word.

"Did we have to bring food?" I broke the silence between us.

"Looks like. I didn't know. Frankly, I'm surprised that *jackass* even mentioned it after all we've been through, Son."

"Are we going to the hospital?"

"Yes, but later. It's okay if Greg thinks we're going right now."

"You told him we are having lunch."

"Relax, Ishmael, and don't tell you mother about this, please."

"So, what *is* for lunch?"

"Your mother made lasagna."

I knew better than to remind him that my mother also knew we were supposed to be having lunch at the Church. Plus, it was information I'd heard on the phone call to which I shouldn't have been privy. I guess tyrants can succumb to the depths of shame and embarrassment – and another rare human moment from my father.

It didn't hit me right away, but something else was on my mind. Greg asked what my dad brought for the potluck. My sister could have died, but he asked about our dish. It made me wonder how much my father's boss really, *truly* cared.

Part II: Chapter Three

I spent the rest of that Sunday expecting Sarah to return home with my mother, but when Dad left the house and my mother came back, it was evident Sarah would not be coming back for some time.

The following morning, my mother woke me up for school. I went downstairs and ate my cereal in complete silence. Mom said nothing about Sarah, and I decided not to ask.

When she did finally speak, it was about something different altogether. "Don't worry about catching the bus this morning. Take your time – I'll drive you to school."

"Why?" I asked her.

"It's been a tough weekend for you." Mom smiled at me. "How about I drive you there *and* back?"

The conversation seemed innocent enough, but I remember it as being one of the most pivotal moments of my life and a true test of my character: On one hand, I relished the opportunity to spend time with my mother when she wasn't venting her pent-up frustrations on me. I truly loved my mother, regardless of the pain and suffering she caused me. I sympathized and always saw her as a fellow victim of the world and circumstance. On the other hand, I was scared at the thought of having the other kids at school see her. She was black, which was bad enough in a town like Ashford, but worse for being married to a white man.

The guilt inside me reached a boiling point. I did my best to conceal it but couldn't escape my mother's fine-tuned perception.

"Don't worry, honey… I have to go to the pharmacy. I'll drop you off a block before school so I don't have to stick around – that's hard with all the Monday-morning buses and cars. Come on."

Doing as instructed, I joined Mom in the car. I didn't even look at her for the first five minutes of our trip. I wasn't avoiding her, I just had nothing to say.

We came to a halt at a red light.

"Ishmael? Ishmael? *Isshy*?" Mom broke into my thoughts.

"Yah?"

"Honey, you know I love you, right?"

"Umm… yah…"

"I know it's strange for you to hear that, and I guess that's my fault – and your father's. Look, we both love you so much, and we love Sarah exactly the same. I never thought something so bad could happen to our family, but that's what God does, and I can't argue with His logic, can I?"

"No, because He's God," I said.

"Right, baby. And I know how hard your life is in this terrible town. I know it doesn't seem like I know anything about what you're going through, but I do. And, believe it or not, so does your father."

"He's mad a lot," I ventured.

"I know," Mom said with a sad frown. "But that's because he doesn't know how to raise a child in the world we live in; it's a mean, unpredictable place. He just doesn't have it in him. I do know school is hard for you, right? The kids pick on you?"

"Yeah."

"Don't be so mad at Daddy. He does know. But he also knows that if you do well in this school, we can send you to a better school later on so you can make a lot of money when you grow up. He just doesn't want you to end up like the other kids."

"They make fun of me for being black. They even make fun of you."

"Because Mommy is a *nigger*?"

"Don't say *that word*, Mom!" I was shocked to hear it from her mouth.

"No baby, it's okay. It's not the first time I've heard that nasty word, and I'm sure it won't be the last. I've been hearing it my entire life. Listen, it's okay to feel bad. Any boy with a heart and soul feels awful when folks say horrible things about his family. Just remember this: If you take their shit today, you will take their shit forever. But if you take things too far, they'll take you away. I can't tell you how to get bad people to stop hurting you in a town like this, but what I can say is to think of those kids as nothing more than a chore, a distraction to overcome. Nothing more than a dog barking while you're trying to watch television. Do you understand?"

"I think so."

"Do you bark back when dogs bark at you?" Mom asked.

"Nope."

She looked at me with happy approval.

"Well, looks like we're close to your school. Can you walk from here?"

"Yeah."

"Okay. I love you, Sweetie."

I smiled at Mom, got out of the car, and walked the last block to school.

I will never forget that conversation with my mother. It was the first time she'd ever acknowledged my right to demand self-respect – except she'd missed a key detail. She had separated the actions of my father and the kids at school from her own, but she was no angel either. She'd said so many hurtful things to me when she got mad, none of which I'd ever forget. I knew she didn't really mean them, but at what point would I stop taking shit from *her*?

I walked into Mr. Janicek's class. While I was reasonably certain he knew about Sarah, I didn't know how much the rest of the class knew. I sat down at my desk in the corner with eleven minutes to go until class started. Brett and Mark saw me, and I just *knew* they were thinking up their morning insults for me. I guess they had no idea about Sarah; it was actually better that way.

"Hey, *Pissmael*!" I didn't look up to see which of the two said that.

"Don't start," I warned. An aura of newfound confidence embraced me, thanks to the severity of Sarah's situation. I'd experienced the worst. Now these fuckers as school seemed miniscule.

"Ya gonna piss your pants today?"

"Why do you want to know?" I asked slowly.

"Because I need to know if I should move desks already. You're gross," said Mark.

"Why wait for it to happen? If you're scared of piss, then just move," I snapped back.

"Ughh, Pissmael just said he's gonna piss his pants!" Mark announced loudly to the class.

"*Mark! Brett!* One more outburst like that and I'll write you both up!" Mr. Janicek hollered.

Then, in the background, with the most faint and gentle voice, I heard Erin. "Eww, he's always *so* gross." Now I had it. Did she actually have the audacity to talk shit about me after what I'd done to her?

"What did you say?" I demanded out loud.

No one responded, although I stared right at Erin. Immediately, she began her innocent routine, but I wasn't having it.

"I'm talking to you, Erin. Did *you* just call *me* gross?"

"What's he talking about?" Erin asked the class in her sweetest, most innocent voice.

"Ishmael, calm down," said Mr. Janicek.

I didn't listen to him.

"*You* called *me* gross?" I repeated for emphasis. "Let's talk about last week."

"Huh?"

"We all know why you were called to the office, and it wasn't because of the A/C!"

"Ishmael! *one more word* and I'll end this myself," Mr. Janicek yelled, his face reddening.

I kept my gaze locked on Erin for another few moments before looking away. I didn't need to say a word: She could hear me telepathically call her a *bitch* with the conviction in my eyes.

I decided at that juncture it was within my best interest to hold back. I didn't mention the smell, but Erin knew what I was talking about.

And that was enough.

As Mr. Janicek began the lesson, I took every opportunity to catch Erin's eyes again. I hadn't chosen her as my target for intimidation because she was a small girl and therefore an easier target. I'd grown up believing women to be immensely powerful and no less terrifying than men. I'd simply picked Erin, not Brett or Mark, because even though she was the one who'd left the class because she had shit in her hair, she still felt entitled enough to call me gross. It was as if her situation was more justified than mine due to some natural birthright. Throughout the morning, Erin glanced cautiously toward me to see if I was looking at her.

I made sure she was never disappointed.

***

Walking home after school that day, I caught sight of a shadow on the sidewalk that looked as if it was trying to catch up to me. It had a beautiful outline and moved with so much grace

I slowed my step.

"Hi, Ishmael!"

"Hi, Claire."

"I heard about your sister being in the hospital."

"Really? I didn't tell anyone."

"My mom works in the hospital. She saw you there and asked if I knew you."

"Oh, well yeah, Sarah's really sick."

"I feel really bad for you… having to go through that."

"It's okay. I'm sure she'll be alright."

"Are you going to go visit her?"

"Yeah, when my dad goes next."

We reached the end of my street. The left took me to my house, and to the right was a wooded area protected from future land development because of some rare mushroom, or protected fancy bird, or some shit. I didn't know.

"Can I show you something?" Claire gestured toward the trees.

"Umm… okay. Will it take long?" I didn't want to incur my parents' wrath by getting home late.

"Not that long."

Claire took my hand and led me into the woods. It wasn't scary at all; the trees were spaced out and the sparse canopy allowed sunlight to warm the ground. A little deeper in and the trees provided privacy from the street.

"I've never been in here before," I told Claire. "What are you showing me?"

"I wanted to tell you something first," Claire said with a knowing smile. "I know you're smart, Ishmael."

"We aren't in the same class. How do you know that?"

"I just *know* stuff like that. I also know how mean the kids are to you, and it makes me really sad."

"Really?"

"Yeah. I can't stand up for you because I don't have a nice home either, and if I do, my dad might find out I like someone who is… umm."

"Who is what?"

"Black."

"That's not your fault. But… you *like* me?"

"Maybe." Claire's cheeks turned tomato-red.

"So… can we be boyfriend and girlfriend?"

"I don't know about that stuff, but please don't tell anyone," Claire pleaded.

"I won't. I like you too, Claire. Let's keep it a secret."

"Okay, but we need to have a place to keep our secrets."

"Is that why we are in the woods?"

"Let's make a place to keep our secrets, Ishmael. Right here, under this tree. Let's dig a hole and keep our secrets in it."

"How can I dig –?"

"You can use that shovel." Claire pointed to a rusty old shovel propped up against a nearby tree. Half of the blade was in the dirt, buried after many years of rain.

"Okay."

"Dig, Ishmael. I want to watch you."

I grabbed the yellow handled shovel and stabbed into the soft ground. The soil was loose. I dug for a while, making a hole about two feet deep and around four feet in diameter.

"Do you think it's deep enough to hold all our secrets?" Claire asked.

"Yeah. This is enough."

"No, Ishmael, let me help you make it deeper."

Claire stood behind me and placed a soft hand on top of mine. We both held the shovel and dug; our combined strength made the task even easier. I lost track of how much time went by, but before I knew it, the hole was another two feet deeper with a diameter of at least five feet; a tall mound of dirt surrounded the perimeter and I thought it resembled a castle's walls.

Finally, Claire took her hands off mine and looked right at me.

"I want to be here for you when people tease you, or for your sister, *anything*. Just keep it a secret, okay?"

I nodded yes.

Claire looked into my eyes, put her arms around me, and kissed my cheek. Then, she grasped the air next to my cheek with her right hand and tossed into the hole.

"That's our first secret, Ishmael! Now it's safe."

"Yay!"

"Okay, I have to go. Alone."

I considered trying to talk her out of it, but Claire walked away briskly towards the street before I could get a word out.

I walked after her, but she reached the sidewalk while I was still in the woods; she didn't acknowledge me at all.

While I still had no real grasp on what had just happened between us, I guessed there might just be some hope in the God-forsaken world after all.

Part II: Chapter Four

The next day at school was the beginning of an experience I'd never expected.

Within fifteen minutes of class starting, A.P. Brown pulled me out. I walked into the front office to find a bunch of the administrative staff waiting for me.

"Hello, Ishmael," they said in unison.

"Hi," I said, not sure where to direct my greeting.

"Ishmael," one of the counselors began – she was new to the school, and I had no idea what her name was. "We really need some help and don't know who we can trust. Mr. Janicek said it would be good idea to ask you."

"What do you need me for?"

"We need a little help with the second-grade classes. We have the test schedule for next week – could you help us make sure each test is legible? The Xerox machine has been acting up."

"Sure, I can do that," I told her. Normally, I'd be smart enough to know it was merely a ruse for something else, but the feeling of being accepted, needed, clouded my intuition.

And so, I sat there in the office for the next half hour or so and went through every test package. Eventually, Principal Labar came back and told me to go back to class. "I'll finish the rest on my own," he said, handing me a frozen yoghurt gift certificate as a thank you for my hard work.

When I walked into the classroom, no one gave me the usual look of disgust or shied away as if I carried some terrible, contagious disease; there was not one derogatory remark. The boys simply ignored me, and some of the girls had a look of sympathy on their face. I wasn't accustomed to being treated with anything other than derision, so it was obviously very strange for me.

Before I knew it, it was lunchtime.

I sat at my broken desk in the corner and ate lunch without anything being thrown at me. Mrs. Allen still watched over me like a hawk, but looked away the second I made eye contact with her. I looked around the lunchroom to find Claire, but she was nowhere to be seen. I knew she'd be there somewhere, and I remembered our agreement to keep us a secret. It would have been enough for me to have just seen her face just once, but knowing we were in the same lunchroom was enough for me.

After lunch was Mr. Janicek's science class. I always enjoyed the subject and my grades had improved dramatically after I'd learned to live in my own mind. The lesson's subject was astronomy and at the beginning, Mr. Janicek told us about a contest NASA was running.

"The majestic Earth, the third rock from the Sun, by chance lies in a habitable zone warm enough to maintain liquid water and an atmosphere. Among our planet's other wonders is a magnetic field shielding its surface from harmful solar radiation," Mr. Janicek told us.

I sat and listened intently as my teacher implied such chance occurrences *had* to be a blessing from a higher power – otherwise life simply would not exist.

"Imagine class, this place we call home is the *perfect* distance from the Sun. The Earth also has an iron and nickel core that generates a magnetic field so we are protected from cosmic and solar radiation. We have just the right gases in the air to make photosynthesis possible and allow us to breathe! However, there are some lesser-known phenomena that allowed life on Earth. Does anyone know what part Jupiter played in the formation of life on Earth?"

The class seemed genuinely confused. I chose not to speak up.

"Nobody? Well, our solar system is not alone in the universe. There are many meteors and comets orbiting the Sun in erratic orbits. Therefore, there is always the risk, although small, that there could be a collision. Jupiter's gravity is so strong that it actually pulls many of these objects away from us! Because of that, I hope you can all see how incredibly lucky we are to live on Earth."

I couldn't take it anymore.

I raised my hand.

"Yes, Ishmael?"

"Mr. Janicek, I don't think that's a blessing at all. It's just something that happened."

"That was my point, Ishmael. If none of those things had happened, we wouldn't be here to enjoy life."

"I understand that, but I don't think it's a *blessing* –"

"Ishmael, must you disrupt my class every time?"

"No, I don't mean disrespect you, but you said it was class discussion time. I want to contribute, and you have a sign on the wall that says *'all ideas considered'*."

It was true: there was a sign made out of shiny silver construction paper. My teacher had been caught in his own fallacy about my intentions. Thus, he had no option but to allow me to continue, although he did not sound very happy about it.

"Okay, Ishmael, fine. Say whatever it is you wanted to say."

"Well," I began. "I know a lot of stuff had to happen for the Earth to support life, but I don't think it's a *blessing*. It's just something that happened, and if it didn't happen, we wouldn't even know about what could have been. I think things are *blessings* and stuff if they make things better. But if something just *happens*, that's why we have reality in the first place. Also, why just Earth? Wasn't the formation of our Sun a blessing too? What about when the solar system was created? What about the Big Bang? Surely *that* was a blessing? I don't think so because if things were different, Earth wouldn't have life, we wouldn't be here, and we wouldn't be able to say Earth didn't make life, so that's *not* a blessing. Suppose I wanted a new bike and my parents got it for me. That's a blessing because if I didn't get it, I can see that —"

"Ishmael, *enough*!" Mr. Janicek cut me off. "I've let you speak, but now you're just acting up to impress the girls."

The embarrassment hit me like a brick.

The guy had been kind to me only the week before, and I'd started believing he may have empathized with me and my miserable lot in life — but then *that* outburst. He'd only mentioned girls to force me into submission and divert the fact he'd been beaten by a kid. His ammunition was accurate, and he knew I couldn't tell my parents about his bullying. So, I sat there at my desk and cried with no tears.

I'd learned something that day: Being evil is innate, and any change to that is only temporary.

I went home that evening with my backpack much heavier than usual. I had a lot of homework that evening and wanted to get started right away. I'd decided to enter the NASA contest. After my encounter with Mr. Janicek, I felt I might be able to prove him wrong again. I'd been pretty fucking embarrassed by his comment about impressing the girls in the class, but I also understood how I'd outsmarted him to make him say something like that.

I perused the question on the entry flyer:

Where does our Solar System end and interstellar space begin?

If you think you know the answer, enter the Science Olympiad writing essay! Five-page limit, double spaced. Illustrations and diagrams welcome but extra points won't be awarded for them. They are only to illustrate points made in the paper. First prize is $1,000 and a week in Houston with NASA.

I thought it was strange how the comment about the illustrations was in the main instructions and not some fine print. It just looked off to me. Who wrote that flier?

Regardless, I was very excited about writing the essay because I happened to know a lot about the topic. Plus, the essays wouldn't be judged by the pious schools, but by NASA engineers. That would show Mr. Janicek and the rest of the stupid school.

"What's that, Ishmael?" Mom asked as I walked through the door.

"It's a flyer for a Science Olympiad writing contest. It's about the solar system. If I win, I get to visit NASA."

"You do know a lot about space," Mom looked impressed. "Will you have the time with all your *real* school work?"

I nodded. "It's due after Christmas break, so it won't affect school," I reassured.

"Okay. Be sure to do a good job. Now, go upstairs and check on Sarah."

"Wait, what? She's home?" I could barely believe my ears.

My mother's only response was a smile.

It felt too good to be true!

I ran upstairs and looked around for her, but she was nowhere to be seen. Surely a two-year-old girl couldn't stay so silent?

I checked in Sarah's room, under her crib, but she was nowhere to be seen. I went to my parents' bedroom and looked under the bed and in their closet.

My sister wasn't there, either.

I was about to check the bathroom when I heard the faintest sound coming from my room. Why hadn't I thought of that earlier?

In my room, everything seemed to be in order. Suddenly, one of my pillows moved ever so slightly.

Pretending not to notice, I closed the distance between myself and the bed. There, I grabbed the top pillow and yanked it away.

My little sister was hiding beneath it; she erupted in laughter, delighted at being found.

I pulled Sarah off the bed and cradled her in my arms. Damn, I loved nothing more in the world than my sister; her deep brown eyes, curly brown hair, her chubby-yet-adorable body, and her innocent, girly smile.

"I was hiding and you *finded* me!" she trilled.

"Yes, I found you, sweetheart." I held Sarah tight and kissed her soft cheek. "You know Sarah, so many people are mean to me, but you're always so nice and sweet. I love you so much," I whispered.

"I love brother too!" Sarah yelled in my ear. "Take me to Barbie!"

I carried my little sister to her room, where she sat in the middle of the floor and walked Barbie around like some comical stop-motion animation. I watched her for a little while before heading to my room; it was the first day of Christmas break, and all I could think of was writing that Science Olympiad essay.

I spent the next week studying articles and learning all about solar wind and cosmic radiation. Many students would make the argument that our solar system ends with Pluto, but I knew different. And, since I had no friends, except maybe

Claire, the essay was my only priority – fueled by Mr. Janicek's cruel insult and my genuine interest in astronomy.

And, as I applied my mind to our planet, all of humankind's problems – from something minor like forgetting to take a pencil to class to major issues like infanticide, murder, rape, and war – I realized were nonexistent beyond our minuscule blue marble. Exploring the rings of Saturn, imagining a trip on a comet, walking on the surface of Mars, or simply strolling on the surface of the Moon would take me away from all of Earth's drama and injustice. The Earth and all its conflicts became insignificant to me.

Saturday night, as I lay in bed staring at the full moon and the Sea of Tranquility, I heard my door open.

"Hi, Iss," Sarah said.

"Hi, Sarah."

"What you doing?" she asked inquisitively; she looked perplexed at seeing her big brother just staring out of the window and doing nothing.

"Looking at the Moon," I told her.

"How come the Moon is all up and not *falled* down?" she asked me. It was an impressive question for someone so young. How could I possibly explain it in terms she'd understand?

"My little monkey, it's something called an *orbit*." Technically, things in orbit *are* falling down, but I didn't want to confuse or frighten my sister. I had to tread with caution.

"I heard that word before." Sarah puffed out her chest, clearly proud of herself for knowing such a clever word.

"Orbit happens in space. It's when one object goes around another object. In this case, the moon is in orbit around the Earth."

"Yeah, but it doesn't *falled* down," Sarah pressed.

She was young, and thus her perception of reality was only what she could see from her own point of view. The moon revolves around the Earth, and that makes sense using the universe as a baseline perspective. However, when the surface of the Earth is the baseline, it makes sense that the moon *has* to fall down.

"Okay, Monkey – I know it's a little hard to understand, but later this week, we can sit down and I'll draw it out for you. Okay?"

Sarah seemed disappointed. "Okay," she grumped. "Can you take me to bedtime?"

Picking Sarah up, I carried her – airplane style – to her bed; she giggled the whole way there. I tucked her in, kissed her cheek, and turned out the light.

Returning to my room, I began writing the paper.

I made the argument that the true edge of our solar system is the point at which the Sun's influence on the universe in terms of radiation is equal to the universe's influence on the solar system. The concept was not new, but opinions varied, and I was taking a side.

I worked diligently on that paper over the next three days; my parents pretty much left me to it, although they'd occasionally enquire as to how things were going. They wanted me to do well. However, they never asked how I *felt*. I guessed that, to their way of thinking, I had become a complete person: The legitimacy of a child was based on academic performance and ambition. Meet those criteria and you're a human being worthy of kindness and respect.

The *human* title meant very little.

The day before the end of Christmas break, I was finally done with my essay – and damn proud of it, too!

I gave it to my dad to mail in and pretty soon forgot about all it. While the prospect of winning had excited me at first, the fact I was finally finished excited me more. I'd particularly enjoyed the nights where I'd worked while Sarah sat next to me on the bed and played quietly with her dolls. We didn't interact much – we didn't really have to; my little sister and I were just so happy to be with each other.

February 1st

"Ishmael!" Dad's yell filled the house. "There's a letter for you from NASA!"

"Coming, Dad!" I flew down the stairs.

"What does it say?" my father asked, impatient.

Opening the letter, I read it silently to myself... then all went black.

I woke up from my dead faint to a dull, throbbing pain in the back of my head and my family standing over me as I lay on the couch. A bag of ice rested behind my head.

I'd actually *won* the Science Olympiad and was to travel to Houston, Texas to spend a week with the NASA engineers. Mom and Dad were overjoyed and immediately planned a celebratory dinner at my favorite restaurant.

That night, I showered and was getting ready for my dinner outing. As I was choosing my pants, I heard my father call me.

"Ishmael! Can you get my wallet from the car on the driveway? I'm not dressed yet."

"I'm going now!" I yelled back.

I pulled on my favorite black pants, took the car keys from the counter, and retrieved Dad's wallet from the car. It looked eerie outside: the sky was crystal clear, the moon's silver light glowed upon the cold ground. It may have been just a chunk of rock mindlessly orbiting our planet, but I imagined it was watching us, judging us, and I wondered if it was disappointed with the human race.

Cold, I went back inside but couldn't lock the front door. I wasn't sure if it was broken or not, but I knew the house wasn't secure.

"Dad? The door's not locking," I called to my father, who was glued – as usual – to the evening news. "I turned it hard but it won't lock."

"Yeah, I'll be there in a minute."

"Can you look at it *now*? The door's unlocked, and you said that's not safe."

"I told you I'll come in a goddamn minute!" Dad barked. "Do you have to ruin the night already?" It was the same thing every single night; he just *had* to keep up with every detail of the news – even if it had no impact on his life. It was as if what was going on in his own son's life wasn't important.

"It's dark outside, and I can't lock it –"

"*Shut up!*" Dad shouted. "If you want to go out, you need to just shut the fuck up. I said I'll do it, and I'll do it!"

Pissed off, I walked away and didn't give the door any more consideration.

I went upstairs to my room and read a book as I waited for the evening news to finish so we could head out to the restaurant. I'd chosen Chester's Funtime Shack. I knew me and my sister would have to share just twenty dollars' worth of tokens to play the games and then be subjected to a lecture from our parents about how things cost money, but fuck it – that was as normal to us as the air we breathed.

I'd barely read a page of my book when my mom came in. "Ishmael, have you seen Sarah? I'm getting sick and tired of her hide and seek games. The last time, it took me over thirty minutes to find her." Mom huffed and rolled her eyes like it was somehow all my fault.

I shrugged my shoulders. "I don't know where she is, but I'll find her."

And so, I checked under each bed in every room; Sarah was not hiding beneath any of them. I then looked under each and every pillow before looking in all of our closets. I began to grow concerned: It was not like Sarah to be anywhere other than those three favorite hiding places. Not wishing to alarm my parents, I went downstairs and checked every place I could think of.

Suddenly, a shadow moved behind the couch. Relieved, I slowly crept up behind it, careful not to make a sound. Then, I sprang over the couch in a friendly ambush and yelled, *"Hey you little monkey!"*

My relief was short-lived.

The shadow was the potted plant on the windowsill; a car had gone by outside, its lights giving the illusion of movement.

Panic gripped me.

"Ishmael, where is your sister?" Mom asked me, her tone accusatory.

"I can't find her anywhere." Panic filled my voice. "I've looked all over the house – she's nowhere!" I tried to hold it back, but a single tear formed and rolled down my face.

"*What?* She's *lost?*"

Dad turned off the television to join in. "Ishmael! *Where is your sister?!*"

"I don't know," I cried. "I didn't see her anywhere."

"You stupid little *shitty* kid. How many times have I told you –"

"*Samuel!*" Mom screamed. "Shut up, you stupid bastard! We don't have time for that right now. We have to look everywhere!"

Without the TV on, the house was eerily quiet; it made the situation far more tense.

I remembered there was just enough space under the couch for a girl of Sarah's size to crawl under and get stuck.

Maybe she was there.

She was not.

I decided to check the upstairs again. I realized I'd been expecting Sarah to jump out when I found her, but what if she'd fallen asleep somewhere? If she had, it was quite possible I'd miss her.

The silence in the house was suddenly broken. I heard the screech of tires from outside. It sounded like a large vehicle had come to a complete stop; I guessed it was at the stop sign six houses away on the corner of Hazelnut Drive and Benders End.

At the top of the stairs, I heard a sound outside again.

An engine revved, a vehicle accelerated quickly. I peeked out through the landing window and, in the dark outside, caught sight of the tail-end of a black pick up roar past our house. It was odd for any vehicle to race along our quiet road – drivers always paid attention to the *"Please Drive Slow – We Love Our Children"* signs.

Something told me I should check the front door.

Running down the stairs, I saw our front door was not closed all the way. I had no time to think. Acting on pure instinct, I pulled the door open and stormed out toward the stop sign on Hazelnut and Bender.

As I walked four houses down, I suddenly realized I had no idea why I was outside; it felt like I was a spectator in someone else's dream.

Preparing to walk back to my house with the slightest hope my parents had not noticed my absence when I was supposed to be looking for my sister, I noticed a tiny white light illuminating a small patch of crabgrass by Miss Cherub's yard. It looked to me like a flashlight. Walking over, I bent over the pick up the mysterious object and, upon recognizing it, my knees gave way.

I collapsed to the ground and felt my bladder let go.

It was Sarah's *GirlsTime* camera – a simple device that printed crude, highly pixelated pictures on small squares of special photo paper.

Composing myself, I got back to my feet and instinctively walked over to the stop sign. There, what appeared to be a bundle of clothes in the middle of the street was slowly moving toward the curb. Then, the bundle moved under a street light.

A white coat and red boots.

They looked like Sarah's.

Panic clenched my chest, my heart pounded, and I ran to the bundle.

I knelt down next to the tiny bundle.

It *was* Sarah.

Running on pure adrenaline, I carried my sister's broken body to the grass and sat down to cradle her in my arms. Her legs were shattered, one side of her head was crushed and pouring with blood that covered her beautiful face apart from beneath her eyes – her tears had washed some of the blood away. Limp in my arms, Sarah gasped for air.

"Sarah?" My voice trembled. "Why are you outside, Monkey?"

Her eyes met mine and she struggled to speak. "I go outside… to… take picture… for you… for win space…"

I knew exactly what she meant.

"Iss, it hurt."

"I know, Monkey, but we'll get you all better. I know it hurts, but you are so strong. You'll be just fine, Monkey," I said softly, holding back tears. I was pretty fucking good at that.

"Iss?"

"Yes?'

"It *really* hurts..."

My little sister closed her eyes and died in my arms right there under the streetlight. I buried my face in her tiny, shattered body. Then, I used my sleeve to wipe away the blood from her precious face. She was still beautiful.

With her face clean, I kissed my sister's cheek over and over, and told her I loved her, hoping against hope for a reply.

One never came.

Her sweet face, bloodied and broken, looked at peace; it was as if she'd passed away with no fear or pain while in the presence of angels.

My entire world had disappeared as my only happy reality was the bundle I held in my arms; thus, I didn't notice at first the loud scream from only three feet away. I looked up and saw my mother and my father.

"Oh my God!!" Mom's horrified voice filled the dark street. *"What happened?!"*

"I found her, Mom," I cried. "She died just now," I cried.

My mother's screams were so loud, shrill, filled with agony that all the houses on our street sprang to life: lights turned on, and our neighbors made their way over to us.

Part II: Chapter Five

I have never spoken about my sister's funeral, and I don't intend to start now. I think of myself as a man of great dexterity and resilience, but not much has changed since the day I watched Sarah's small coffin lower into the ground surrounded by my family, friends, and my father's acquaintances.

For the few weeks following Sarah's death, my classmates left me alone. A handful of teachers offered me their condolences, but that didn't feel as good as being able to sit in my broken desk in the corner of the lunchroom and eat in peace. More than ever, if given the chance to sit among my peers and be accepted as one of them, there was no chance in hell I'd ever choose to do so. The town has already taken so much from me.

On one day of no particular significance, I was sitting in the lunchroom refusing to eat. All attempts to keep Sarah out of my mind were futile, so I approached Mrs. Allen and asked if I could spend the next few days in the library.

"I don't believe that's for me to decide, young man," Mrs. Allen grumbled. "Did you ask Mr. Janicek?"

I shook my head. "You're the lunch monitor - I thought you had to give me permission."

"Don't make assumptions, Ishmael. That's irresponsible and rude. Do I make myself clear?" And that was Mrs. Allen being *nice*.

"Yes, Ma'am."

"Stay here for today," she sighed. "I'll ask Mr. Janicek about you starting tomorrow." She then pointed at the broken desk like I was a disobedient dog.

The next day, Mr. Janicek approached me in the classroom before lunch.

"Why are you not eating, Ishmael?" he asked.

"I can't eat, and I'd throw up if I did," I explained, my lower lip quivering.

"I guess under the circumstances it'll be okay for you to spend lunchtime in the library." My teacher sounded most sympathetic. "I will have to inform your parents that you're not eating, though."

I had no problem with that.

Fuck them.

When the lunch bell rang, I went to the library and sat myself down. The room was bright and warm but it still felt incredibly desolate. The air was still, the sound from the AC vents was barely audible, and the lights showed not even the slightest flicker.

I liked it - the library mirrored how I felt inside.

Calm, constant.

I wandered along the aisles of books in the hope of something to pique my interest. There were plenty of educational books, of course: the Great Pyramids of Giza, the secluded tribes of the Amazon, the Great Wall of China... All very interesting, but I really wasn't in the mood to learn about past civilizations and geography.

So, I moved over to the medical books in the science section. Nothing much there, either. I was about to give up and just sit quietly when a particular book caught my eye.

It was a medical book aimed at mid-graders: *Diabetes*.

Given the book's subject matter, there was no apparent need for flare: straight to the point. I figured someone wouldn't want to read a book about diabetes in the same manner in which one would read a Stephen King novel. Regardless, my interest was aroused because my parents had told me about blood sugar and why it was important.

I took the book to a desk at the back of the library and began reading from the beginning. However, I didn't get too far because the bell rang. I headed off to class.

The rest of the day went without incident. I wasn't called *Pissmael*. I wasn't harassed. But best of all, I didn't have to sit in the lunchroom at my broken table while being eyed down by that bitch.

That evening, the second I got home from school, my mother asked me why she'd gotten a call telling her I wasn't eating at school. I tried to talk to her but choked up.

"It's fine with me, Ishmael, I do understand why you don't feel like eating," Mom soothed. "Just try not to waste your time while you're in the library. Read something. Maybe do some homework so you'll have less to worry about at home."

I looked away from my mother. She knew I was hurting. With Sarah's death, I wouldn't go so far as to say I felt strengthened, but I was definitely more durable and accepting of any misfortunate that might come my way.

"Something on your mind, Ishmael?" Mom asked.

"No."

"Look at me," she insisted. I obliged, and Mom raised her eyebrows at me.

"I'll do my homework when I get home," I told her.

"Why waste an opportunity like that?"

"Because if I don't have homework to do, Dad will think I'm doing nothing," I told her the truth. "And he will force me to study anyway. I don't need to do that *all* the time. I don't want to do anything I don't have to when I come home. At least if I save my homework, he'll think I'm busy."

"I know how you feel, but your father cares about your future, and I don't think he deserves such disrespect from you."

"Whatever…"

"Ishmael, I know you're going through a lot, but don't take it out on the parents who love you. Do you understand me?"

"Sure."

"Now go to your room, unwind, and come down for dinner when I call you."

"Okay." I did as instructed. Maybe she'd tell Dad what I'd said about him, maybe she wouldn't. Either way, I didn't care. What could he do? Hit me?

I was free of fear.

After my sweet little sister died in my arms, what else was there to be scared of?

For the next two weeks, I continued with my routine of having lunch in the library. I finished the book about diabetes and began reading a book about the body's muscular system.

One boring day, I sat reading with my back turned to the rest of the library. I was learning about the muscular and skeletal systems when I heard light footsteps behind me. Turning around, I found myself looking right into the most beautiful eyes in the world.

"Hi, Ishmael," said Claire.

"Oh, hi," I replied.

"I didn't see you at lunch for a long time. I didn't know you'd be in here."

"I decided to have lunch in the library – I don't feel much like eating."

"Is it about your sister?" Claire asked. Her eyes closed a little, her eyebrows raised, and her bottom lip pouted as if she was genuinely sad for me.

"She died a few weeks ago." I struggled to get the words out.

"I heard about it. Can I sit with you?"

"Sure."

Claire sat herself down beside me.

"How come *you're* here?" I asked her.

"I'm not hungry, and I don't feel good. This week isn't good for me, either."

"Is everything okay?" It was my turn to be concerned. She *looked* fine to me, but that wasn't to say she didn't have emotional turmoil going on.

"Yeah, I'll be better in a week. In the meantime, they said I can come here at lunchtime."

"Well, I'm happy you're here," I told her.

"Me too." Claire smiled at me. "Now I don't have to be alone. I'm very sorry everyone teases you, Ishmael. I see it all the time, but can't say anything to help because my dad doesn't like black people. I can't make him angry because that gets him mad at me."

"It's okay," I sighed. "I remember when we talked about it. I just ignore it. The bullies are just jerks, I guess."

"They're so mean to you for no reason."

I shook my head; they did have a reason – a good one. "It's because I'm a *nigger* just like my mom."

"My dad says that word, but I don't think the color of someone's skin should matter," Claire said. "That's why I don't like my dad. Did you know I have an older brother?"

I shook my head again.

"Yeah, he's twenty-five, and I haven't seen him for two years. I really miss him."

"That's *so* old!" I was genuinely surprised.

"Yeah, Dad is in his fifties, and my brother was born a long time ago – we don't have the same mom. Dad got divorced years ago – I heard him and *my* mom fighting once and heard that my brother's mom left because Dad was mean to her and hit her. She was so upset that she left my brother with him and moved to Romania. Then Dad married my mom and they had me."

"How come you don't see your brother?"

"He had a girlfriend for a long time but she never came over; her name was Jana. Then, one day she finally came to visit, and we found out her nickname was Jana. Her *real* name was actually Sanjana. She was Indian."

"That's *so* cool! I saw loads of Indian people in New York."

"She's so pretty and smart – she's a doctor now. Dad was angry before she even had the chance to say hello to him. Dad tried to hit my brother but he is fat and slow. My brother and his girlfriend left. A few days later, I found a letter to me inside the pocket of a dress my brother and Sanjana bought for me. I never showed it to my parents, of course. They told me they loved me and when the time was right, they'd come back for me."

I felt guilty.

Up to that point, I'd elevated Claire in my mind to the level of an angel, but I'd never actually humanized her. When I thought of Claire, I pictured her beautiful face and soft voice, and the way she'd made me feel that night in the woods. I'd never pictured her as a vulnerable person just like me with problems and emotions.

"You haven't talked to him since then?"

Claire gave a sad nod. "I don't know where he went. It's why I feel bad when people say horrible things about you, *to* you. I don't think being black matters, you know?"

"Thank you, Claire."

"So… what are you reading?" Claire leaned toward me a little to nose at my book.

"It's all about muscles." I was unsure as to whether she would assume I was a nerd or appreciate my inquisitive mind and thirst for knowledge.

"That's so cool!" Claire enthused. "I'm reading a book about marine biology. I love the ocean *so much*!"

"My favorite topic is astronomy," I said. "I won that NASA contest."

"I heard Casey Gunter got to go to NASA."

"She was second place. I dropped out because of… you know… my sister."

Claire didn't say anything. Reaching over, she held my hand softly and looked at me in a way that told me I'd never be alone again. After a tender moment or so, she let go and went back to her book.

That's how I spent the remainder of the lunch period. Claire and I sat together and read our books – but *together*. She was so close to me; I smelled her strawberry shampoo and felt the warmth of her breath when she exhaled.

After losing Sarah, I'd lost all hope in my life, but sitting next to Claire gave me a little optimism. For the first time in a long, long time, I felt a reason to believe in good. My thoughts drifted to Erin and Brett. I'd damaged things important to them, and even though they deserved it, I had Claire while they had no such thing. Therefore, I was the one truly blessed. I knew I should look down with empathy on those beneath me; I never thought such a feeling would come to me, but I felt a little guilt for the two I'd hurt.

Claire sat with me in the library for the next week, and then she had to go back to the lunchroom. I returned to my broken desk a week after that when the school counselor told me I *had* to eat lunch. I argued that I *still* had no appetite, but apparently, I needed to be supplied a lunch, whether I ate it or not. – something to do with district policy.

Returning to the lunchroom, I was terrified my broken desk would no longer be there. Much to my relief, it was right where I'd left it.

I sat down with my district-mandated lunch and ate while making eye contact with no one. I wanted to look around for my Claire, but I also didn't want to ruin her social standing by having her associated with the school negro: I cared far too much about her for that.

So, I kept my head low, finished my soggy cheeseburger, and kept to myself. In my own mental universe, I vowed to be a good person to honor the memory of my baby sister. I imagined she was watching everything I did from wherever she was; Claire had given me the confidence to do right by Sarah.

I might have lost my baby sister, but I'd gained two angels.

Part II: Chapter Six

Breakfast was crappy.

My mom had made my favorite: silver dollar pancakes with no syrup, eggs cooked over-medium, and four slices of crispy bacon. No one made breakfast like Mom.

Yet, sitting across the table from Sarah's empty chair was enough to make even my most favorite meal taste like a rabid dog's asshole after a fresh shit.

I simply couldn't enjoy *anything*.

"Just not the same, is it?" Mom observed as she cooked the bacon.

"It's okay –"

"I know it'll never be the same again." My mother was crying, the spatula still in her hand. I jumped out of my chair and ran across the kitchen to give her a hug.

"Don't feel sad, Ishmael," Mom sobbed. "You still have a life to live. Sarah wouldn't want you to be sad all the time, would she?"

"I can't help it. She was my best friend." I cried along with Mom.

"I know, mine too, and Dad's. She was our very own little angel."

After a long, much-needed hug, I returned to the table to finish my breakfast. Mom's eyes were still full with tears, but she'd gotten it under control enough to continue cooking. Seizing the moment, I finally asked the question that had plagued me since my sister died.

"How come Dad never seems like he's sad about Sarah?"

"Why would you ask me something like that? Your sister was his only daughter; imagine how he must feel." She hadn't answered my question, only stated the obvious.

"He doesn't cry or anything," I pressed.

"I know. Your father can seem pretty tough on the outside, but he's not able to express what's in his heart. His love doesn't always feel like love, but it's there. Like with you."

"Me?"

Mom nodded. "I know he comes down tough on you, but that's only because he wants you going out into the world with a full deck – because you're mixed race. There are *so* many horrible people out there. You're a gifted student, and we can't let that go to waste, can we?"

Before I had time to respond, we heard the garage door open.

"Hush up for now, Ishmael. Let's not stress your dad out, okay?"

Sadly, Dad was stressed before he even got into the house.

My father stormed in, pushing the front door open so hard it broke the door stop. He stomped into the kitchen huffing and puffing like an asthmatic dragon. He threw a large cardboard box into the corner of the room.

"Sam, what's going on?" my mother asked.

"*Those goddamn motherfuckers!*" Dad snarled. "Now I know why they asked me to go in an hour late."

"I thought they had a surprise for you," Mom ventured.

"Oh, those redneck bastards had a surprise all right!" Dad screamed as my mother reached inside the dented box and pulled out several wads of cash.

"Sam, what the hell is –"

"*Five thousand dollars!* They raised it for Sarah's funeral expenses." Dad glowered at the money in my mother's hands like it was poison.

"Sam, I know you don't want to take this money, but I'm sure they did what they felt was best. It's okay, we can keep it for now and figure out what to do with it, or how to give it back." She offered a reassuring smile.

"No, Mad, it's what happened before. We don't need to discuss this in front of the boy." He looked at me and pointed toward the stairs.

"Sam, I did nothing to you. Calm down and I'll come upstairs with you to talk. Ishmael, there's extra bacon and pancakes. No more eggs, though."

"That's fine. I want more bacon," I told her. I didn't enjoy the bacon anymore, but it helped thwart my hunger.

My parents went upstairs and I heard their raised voices.

After my extra bacon, I took a peek inside the cardboard box. I'd never seen so much money in my life! Most was bound in tight bundles but some of the bills were loose. Five grand – it was absolutely fucking incredible.

I never forgot my vow to Sarah, nor the inspiration given to me by Claire. I *wanted* to be good person. However, the ends might involve means that weren't always within virtue. I didn't mind that, as I knew I would have no problem hurting someone if it meant defending a loved one. That's how I felt at that moment. As I stared at all that money: someone had done something to upset Dad, and I needed to know what.

I tiptoed up the stairs and approached my parent's bedroom, praying the door would be closed. Finally, some luck – it was closed tight. I stood by it and listened to my parents' conversation, wishing I'd heard the first part.

"…didn't see me in there! I'm not kidding, Mad!" Dad sounded angrier than usual.

"Sam, maybe you didn't hear them correctly."

"You *want* to give them the benefit of the doubt, do you? Those fuckers made me go to work late so they could pray for me. The redneck bastards really said…"

"Said what, Sam?" Mom's voice quivered.

"They said Sarah died because I went against God and made mixed-race babies. They all prayed for us and our souls. The money was more for me than for you, Mad. They prayed I'd find the right path."

Silence for the next minute. I grew worried.

Then, "You bastard, Sam."

"What?"

"Whose idea was it to accept a job in this Godforsaken town? Was this good for our children? I know that's not why we lost Sarah, but the motherfucker who hit her didn't even stop or bother to call the police. Only in a hick town like this!"

"You're blaming me?"

"It was all your idea, Sam!" I heard Mom scream.

"I did what was best for you and our children!"

"How was moving here best for our children? You could have said no and looked for another job – but you dragged us all here knowing your wife is nothing but a *filthy black nigger*!"

"Shut up, Mad." There was sadness in Dad's angry voice. "If I'd ever thought that, why did I marry you?"

"Maybe your attraction to me isn't natural. Maybe you get off on things that are filthy and… *wrong*? Is that why you fucked me and made two children?"

"Watch how you talk to me, Mad!" My father's tone was most threatening. "I've always loved and desired you – because I'm *not* some sick racist. But I'm beginning to I wish I was – I really do, because then I wouldn't have gotten stuck with you!"

Game over.

No way could my father ever take those words back, even though Mom had started that part of the argument.

I ran as quietly as I could to my room and slowly shut the door. I knew my mom would be out of her room to be away from Dad and his hurtful words, and she was. She didn't come to my room, which was good, because I wanted to be alone with my thoughts. I understood all too well what I'd heard: the people of Ashford, Ohio believed my sister's death had been divine intervention. To correct a terrible wrong against God.

Claire's divine beauty and the memory of my sister had made me want to be a better person, but my devotion to that was becoming difficult.

I sat on my bed and relived the last moment my sister was alive in my arms – the moment before she died right there in front of me.

And then I tried to imagine what kind of God would do such a thing just to prove a point.

Part II: Chapter Seven

The next month went by without incident.

I saw Claire a few times in the hallway. As we passed one another, she'd give me a look for a fleeting second. I'd look back, and that was all the connection I needed to inspire me for the day; it felt good to aspire to be a good person.

However, one thing I'd failed to consider was how it was easy to be a good person when your environment isn't out to destroy you.

I've come across so many closed-minded idiots throughout my life who have lived their life, bathed in the blood of the lamb, and devoted their life to the teachings of the Lord – yet they've never experienced poverty, abuse, assault, rape, robbery, or even had a loved one tragically die. Yeah, it's easy to believe in God when you have a life like that. It's as if the Story of Job is conceptual at best, but impossible to consider in a real-life context for the empty-headed.

The broken desk was still my sanctuary during lunch. I even started eating again, and I didn't feel the stares of my classmates degrading me with their gaze while I chewed.

All that changed one day, when none other than Erin – *she of the shitty hairbrush* – approached me. I'd just finished eating, and there was still ten minutes left until class.

"Hey, Ishmael," Erin said quietly. I detected no malice in her voice but remained guarded.

"Hey, Erin," I replied cautiously.

"Umm… I was wondering if you wanted to sit at our table for a minute?"

"You want me to sit with you?"

"Maybe just for a minute?"

"I thought you didn't like me," I said with conviction.

"*Please*, Ishmael," Erin pleaded.

"Sure, why not?" I gave in but kept my wits about me. Even though Erin didn't know the truth about the hairbrush incident, I felt a dominion over her. I was the one who ruined her and made her cry in the nurse's office – *me!* And, although I'd vowed to be a better person, I had the confidence that I could fuck her up again should the need arise.

I walked with Erin over to her lunch table. The other kids there weren't averse to my presence, and I got the feeling it was the beginning of something new. Maybe my good-person pledge was being reciprocated by the forces of the universe? Maybe, just maybe, my desire to be positive and loving wouldn't be a grueling test of emotional and physical dexterity. I didn't know what was about to happen, but it was *definitely* the beginning of something new.

As I sat down, Erin sat next to me. She opened up her schoolbag, pulled out a wad of cash, and handed it to me.

"What is this for?" I was genuinely flummoxed

"It's five hundred dollars… from me and my family," Erin explained. "You know, because of what happened to your sister. We heard all about it from Pastor Lima."

"Your family goes to his church now?" It was all I could think of to say.

"Yeah, we just started going. We heard about what happened and we know God will be happy if I give this to you – so you can be blessed."

"Thank you, Erin, but I don't understand..."

"It's my job to help those who aren't fortunate," Erin told me. "It's not your fault, you know..."

"What isn't?"

"Well, Pastor Lima told us how you were born is not your fault. So, I talked to my parents, and we agreed giving you this will be our good deed for the week."

Had I not eavesdropped on my parents' conversation a few weeks prior, I might have been inclined to view it as a gracious act of kindness. I didn't quite understand the intricate nuances or social hierarchy of Erin's gesture, but I know how I felt: *degraded*.

I stared at the bills in my hand before handing them back to Erin. However, in the spirit of being a good person for Claire and the memory of my sister, I remained gracious.

"Erin, this is really nice of you," I said as Erin's smile widened and her face blushed pink. *Why did such a horrible girl have to be so pretty*? "But I can't take this right now. It's too much money. I'm happy you and your family did this, and I won't forget it."

Erin refused to take the cash so I had to put it on the table. She eyes closed gently and started to sob.

"Erin, no, please don't –"

"I wanted to be a good girl and do something nice because your sister died –"

"I know, but I really can't take this," I reiterated.

Erin's pitiful sobs began to cause a scene and a whole bunch of students looked in our direction, along with Mrs. Allen. Getting up from her seat, she walked over and was immediately drawn to the money. She picked it up.

"Ishmael, what are you paying Erin for?" she asked me.

"No, Mrs. Allen. I was giving it to him because of his sister," Erin explained.

"Oh, sweet girl, don't cry," Mrs. Allen soothed. "I know that was very sad, but if you want to give Ishmael a gift like this, your parents need to call the front office. I'll keep it safe and take it to the principal –we can call your parents so the adults can handle this. Is that okay, sweetie?"

"Ishmael won't take it." Erin's crying grew louder.

"Ishmael, is that why Erin is so upset?"

I nodded. "I just can't take money like that."

"So, you had to be rude and make the poor girl cry?"

"I wasn't rude!" I was close to tears myself. "I was very polite but she started crying! *I was polite!*"

"Look, we all felt terrible when your sister died, and things were turning around for you at school, but now I can see how you bring misfortune on yourself, young man!"

"What *misfortune*?" I said through clenched teeth.

"Maybe because you sit alone so people can't see how cold your heart is?" Mrs. Allen made a crooked smile with her fat, old-crone lips.

"I am not cold at all, I swear. My parents wouldn't allow me to take this money, and I think it's too much. So…"

"Save it, Ishmael," she said loudly; we were now the center of the lunchroom's attention. "You know, I thought you'd open your eyes a little after your sister passed away, but I can see you have no appreciation for the kindness everyone has shown you. Just look around…"

And, in that instant, the relief I'd felt when everyone stopped bullying me was destroyed. My peers' original aversion towards me was renewed – and with vigor. I was once again the puppy who eats from the dog bowl. The stares were disapproving, full of hate and disgust, and condescending.

Mrs. Allen grabbed my shirt collar and lifted me up from my chair. "Come with me," she growled.

'What –?" I tried to speak, but the pressure on my neck was so tight I vomited a little as I was pulled away from the table.

All the kids jumped up in disgust and rushed to the walls of the lunchroom as if there was a fire. Mrs. Allen didn't lessen her hold on my collar and she pulled me out of the room; my shirt lifted up to expose my entire belly and navel as I was dragged away.

Mrs. Allen loosened her grip in the hallway and eventually let me go.

"Fix your shirt," she snapped, as if I *wanted* to walk around in a crop top. I pulled my shirt down and followed her into the empty teacher's lounge.

"Wait here." She had me sit down in the same chair I'd sat in before.

"Why?"

"Erin felt threatened by you – she wouldn't cry for nothing, Ishmael."

I didn't retort. I didn't need to. I knew a closed mind when I saw one.

Mrs. Allen shot me one last look of disapproval and then waddled off. I clenched my fists into a ball and felt the tension in my muscles getting tighter and tighter as my entire body became tense with rage. My teeth chattered as tears poured down my face – only, they were tears of rage, not sadness. Not only did Mrs. Allen lie, she'd talked about my sister…

Losing all control, stood up from the chair. I fell to my knees and screamed into my hands. I expected someone to come but no one did. I balled my fists even harder and prepared to swing at the papers and files upon the wall table, but something caught my eye.

I calmed down immediately, my anger diverted to an inquisitive focus.

The hallway monitors and lunch attendants all had their own individual drawers under the countertop – each one marked by a white label. I looked for the one I knew would be there: *Brenda Allen*. Hers was close to the floor.

No longer scared of consequences, I thought about when I held my little sister as she died, and that gave me conviction. The memory of Sarah's eyes closing during her last breath provided me with strength and dampened my fear. That had been her parting gift to me before leaving me *forever*, and I'd never let a gift from Sarah go to waste.

Drenched in sweat, I opened the cabinet. I had no idea if or when someone from the office might walk in. I found a small insulated bag. Without looking behind me to check if was still alone, I opened the bag and saw something I immediately recognized from the book in the library.

Three vials of insulin nestled beside a cold pack.

I removed one of the vials from the bag; it was cold and condensation immediately formed on the glass. The vial had less liquid in it than the others, the seal broken: Mrs. Allen had clearly used it. I discovered syringes at the bottom of the bag – there were so many, I was certain she wouldn't notice if one was missing. I wasn't sure of what I was going to do next, but my thoughts were interrupted. I looked back toward the door and heard footsteps approaching me; I would never be able to return things to normal in time, and accepted I'd be caught out by a teacher and beaten by my parents.

It was Mr. Janicek.

He walked into the teachers' lounge and straight to the fridge. Because I was on the ground and behind two rows of tables, he didn't see me. Most importantly, he obviously had no reason to expect me to be there.

I sat frozen – so quiet I feared others could hear my heart beat.

As the sting of Mrs. Allen's actions in the lunchroom wore off, I started to consider the consequences. I would be expelled from school if I was caught holding a syringe and a vial of insulin. There was hope Mr. Janicek wouldn't see me, but I figured fixing the crime scene was a safer bet. The drawer was still open, and maybe I could get the items back into Mrs. Allen's bag quietly. Then, if he caught me later, Mr. Janicek likely wouldn't question why I was on the floor sobbing – given what she'd done to me in front of the entire student body.

I needed to take my chances.

Holding my breath, not making a sound, I watched Mr. Janicek grab something from the fridge – a soda of some sort – and sit down at the table furthest from me. As long as I moved very slowly, I knew there was a good chance I'd remain hidden. He'd just opened the can when over the loudspeaker, the principal called for him to go to her office.

I was *so* relieved!

My gut told me his summoning was because of me, but I also knew I had time to get out of my predicament. Mr. Janicek stood up, put his drink down on the table, and walked out of the teachers' lounge.

Alone again, I thought back to what I'd read in the book about diabetes. I poked the syringe's needle through the rubber top of the vial and extracted some insulin. Once the syringe was full, I squirted the contents into the sink.

Looking frantically around the room, I found myself in a worse predicament – I was holding a needle! On the other side of the room, I saw Mr. Janicek's abandoned soda – a can of white grape juice.

I made my move.

I stuck the needle inside the can and filled Mrs. Allen's syringe all the way up – just as I had with the insulin. Then, I injected the grape juice into the vial.

My entire body was shaking and I felt dangerously close to throwing up again – a burning stream of vomit crept up my throat, but I swallowed it down as I repackaged the medical paraphernalia just the way I'd found it and snuck it back in Mrs. Allen's cabinet.

I sat back down. After finding a new moment of clarity, I considered what I'd done; I began to panic at the realization, but reminded myself of my every interaction with Mrs. Allen. The humiliation and the disrespect she'd handed me was too much to bear. I thought of my sister again, and how the ugly old bitch had talked about her.

There was no going back; what was done was done.

A couple minutes later, the bell to the lunch period ended – I didn't dare go back to class without Mrs. Allen's say so. Then, as my fellow students were running around the hallways to get to class, the principal came into the lounge and asked me to go with him to his office.

"Your parents are on the way to discuss the incident with Erin," he told me.

My heart sank; my parents never believed me when given news of my behavior. But I figured sitting down in the same room with them, Mrs. Allen, and the principal would work to my favor. What Mrs. Allen did would have an effect on my parents as it had on me, and I knew they'd *have* to believe me for once.

As we approached the office, Mrs. Allen was just on her way out.

"Leaving us?" asked Principal Labar.

Mrs. Allen shook her head. "I had a cupcake during lunch, so I have to…"

"No, no worries. The Abiases will be here in a while – please be back for that."

"Of course," Mrs. Allen said with a grunt and waddled away.

No going back.

Part II: Chapter Eight

"Explain to me again, Ishmael, so I can understand correctly, because I don't know when Principal Labar will reschedule the meeting," my father said the minute we arrived home.

"Erin gave me the money – I was very polite and said I couldn't take it. Then Erin started to cry and Mrs. Allen dragged me to the teacher's lounge by my shirt collar. It went all the way up and everyone could see my tummy and belly button Then I threw up while she pulled me. She said I scared Erin and I wasn't grateful for people being nice to me after Sarah died." I prayed he'd listen.

"And what caused you to throw up?" asked Mom.

"Mrs. Allen hurt my neck and I threw up."

"Did she take you to the nurse?"

"No, just to the teachers' lounge." I was starting to feel relieved; my parents actually sympathized with me.

"What an irrational, unstable bitch, Samuel. Why the teacher's lounge? Students go in there now?"

"I think it's because taking him to the principal's office would force discipline protocols and Mrs. Allen couldn't defend her rationale against him."

"That *bitch*," repeated Mom.

"Are you sure this Erin said her family heard about Sarah from the new church?" Dad asked me.

"I swear. Pastor Lima."

"Well, we'll definitely get to the bottom of why they suspended you. Meantime, you need to be sure to get all your work done quickly and on-time. I'll speak to the school."

"Okay," I said.

"Good, Son." My father had rare look of love and affection in his eyes. Not something I was normally used to. "Go upstairs now and get some work done."

"I already finished my homework, but I can study," I told him.

"But aren't you already ahead?"

"Yeah, but I'm going to look up SAT words and learn a few a week." Fuck it, I knew when to sell-out.

"It's a little too early to worry about that," Dad grumbled. "But at least you'll learn something useful. Make sure you also peruse the origins of the words. Got it?"

"Sure, Dad." I headed back upstairs. I couldn't believe it: my mom and dad were genuinely on my side! I still felt they wouldn't be had my father not overheard his work's prayer circle. I was grateful he had.

As I neared the top of the staircase, I heard my parents continuing their conversation. Once again, I eavesdropped. Knowledge was power, and I got my first taste of sweet victory.

"She just *collapsed*?" Mom said.

"That's what I heard the principal saying. The fat teacher who did that to Ishmael fell over convulsing in the restroom."

"Where is she now?" asked Mom.

"E.R. She might not make it," said Dad, bluntly.

"My Lord. I don't know what to say."

"I do. If Lima is to be believed in this town, then God has spoken. How dare that woman grab our son like that when he did the right thing? You're right – this town isn't right for us. I'm so sorry, Mad. I *really* am."

"I'm sorry, too – for what I said the other night. I was *disgusting*," Mom said.

"Me too. I don't *really* wish I was racist. I just…"

"I know how much you like Black women, Samuel. Trust me. Let's just forget about it and take care of our son. He's all we have left." Mom's voice choked with emotion.

"I know," Dad said as he began to sob. It felt good to hear that cold-hearted man cry for once.

"Sam, you're a great father in so many ways, but could you please lighten up on Ishmael? He's a gifted student, and I know his education is his ticket out, but he'll be okay. If we don't take care of him today, he won't have a tomorrow."

"You need to watch yourself too, Mad. You're the one who reminds him he shouldn't have been born. Lucky he doesn't know we considered an abortion."

"I know I shouldn't say those things." Mom's voice was subdued. "Jesus knows I have some kind of Hell waiting for me, but I'm not perfect. I love him, Sam. How about *we* work on our son together?"

"Of course, baby. Now come with me…"

"Where are you taking me, Sam?"

"I am pretty sure the backseat will still fit us…"

"Sam?"

I heard them go outside through the front door, and then the car's door open and close. I didn't know what happening, but I got the feeling things would get better for me, at least at home.

And all it had taken was my little sister getting run over by a pickup truck.

Part II: Chapter Nine

My suspension was commuted from three days to only one, and I returned to the school. Mrs. Allen never came back.

I felt no hypocrisy toward my commitment of being a good person. No one blames a judge for sentencing a killer to death. No one blames a lion for killing an innocent zebra to feed her cubs. Well, then why should anyone blame me for bringing justice to a such a foul, disgusting excuse for a human being? Brenda Allen, the epidemy of *vile*, the personification of filth, had finally met justice no differently than if she was arrested for robbing a bank.

It was simply *justice*.

The new hall monitor, Mr. Gracen, was a black man. He was a little older, spoke with a stereotypical southern accent – *howdy suh* – and was developing white hair around the edges. I was relieved to see him. However, there was one problem with Mr. Gracen I had to get over – it all started the day he first spoke to me.

Mr. Gracen had been hall monitor roughly two weeks when he first approached me during lunch.

"How are you, young man?"

"I'm good. How are you?" I replied.

"Can't complain now, can I? Tip top shape," he said, and I laughed politely. "What's your name, son?"

"Ishmael."

"Well, okay then. I am *Mistuh Gracen*. You just let me know if you need anything. Jus' ask me *anything* now."

"Thank you, Sir. I'll do that."

"So then, let me *aks* you a lil sumthin', if I may."

I nodded. "Sure."

"Why ya sitting here on this ol' broken table. This ain't a table for sittin'."

"It's better if I'm alone. No one lets me sit with them," I said sadly.

"Oh, bull honey! Let's see if someone would let you sit with them, shall we now?"

I understood Mr. Gracen's intentions were pure, but it was likely his age that made him think such an idea would end up in my favor. I guessed he was too old to know how awkward and socially damaging it would be for me. I didn't want to throw kindness back, but I *had* to get out of it.

"Let's go now. Come with me, Son."

"No, please, Mr. Gracen. It's a *really* bad idea. I don't want to go."

"You sure?" He backed off a little.

I was afraid some of the nearby kids would hear him, so I knew I had to say something to make him leave me alone while not ruining the rapport I'd built with him. He was suggesting something wrong, but he was still an ally I knew I needed.

"Yes," I said. "You're making me… I mean… that would make me *uncomfortable*." I felt bad for pulling out the word "uncomfortable," but I'd seen how it had the power to make people fall into submission.

Nobody wants to make someone *uncomfortable*.

It was a relief that Mr. Gracen took it so well; he didn't seem offended at all.

"Well okay, Ishmael. Just let me know if you do need me."

"Thank you, Sir."

Smiling warmly, Mr. Gracen – my new friend – walked away, hands in his pockets.

That evening, I went home to find my father waiting for me. He was home so early, and I knew he was there to talk to me.

"You're home already?" I asked, puzzled.

Dad nodded. "I sent your mom out on some errands. Thought maybe we could talk, man to man."

"Okay."

"Son, what do you know what *selling out* means?"

I had no idea what the hell Dad was going on about or where the conversation was headed.

"I've heard the phrase but I don't know what it means."

"Okay... I guess you could say it's when you go against your own morals and beliefs to do the right thing in the end. Do you understand that?"

"Kinda."

"Let me explain: If you don't believe in eating pork, but that's the only food you have left or you die – would you eat it, even though you're not supposed to?"

"If you were gonna die? I would. But *we* eat pork!"

"Shit, okay, bad example." My father paused, thinking. "What about being nice to a mean person so they don't take your house away?"

"I guess I would have to pretend to be nice – because losing our house would be worse," I said.

"See? That's how smart my son is! So, you *do* understand. Well, I wanted to talk to you about selling out. Sometimes parents have to do just that to avoid something worse happening. It's not easy, but sometimes it *must* be done. I know how badly you were treated in school and why that little girl gave you money."

"Erin," I said. "She also makes fun of Mom for being black and married to you."

"I know, and I don't blame you for not taking the money from her. But… you remember how she heard our family needed forgiveness and understanding from Pastor Lima?"

"Yeah."

"Lima is a jerk. A racist, backward jerk. I'm sorry they're talking about us, but you and me are going to continue going to his church."

"Why?"

"Because without my job, we'll be homeless and have nowhere to go. Being seen in Lima's church by my bosses is something I *need* to do. I know it's wrong, but I'm *selling out* because it's best for you and Sar – It's best for you and Mom."

I understood, but only to a small extent. I still figured we really didn't need to go. I felt something that day I'd never felt before: I looked at my father as if he were ten feet tall and ten inches tall at the exact same time. A simultaneous dichotomy, if you will.

"And you know something else," Dad continued. "I sold out somewhere else too – with you. I couldn't help but fall in love with your mom, Ishmael. We had two amazing kids but the world won't accept our love. I'm sorry you're paying the price because we wanted to be together. However, God also made you brilliant, and that's your only ticket out of this dump of a life. They call you *nigger*, don't they? They call Mom *nigger*?"

"All the time," I said as Dad put his arm around me. "But Dad, are you even allowed to say that word?"

"Umm, grey area I guess. But my point is this. Your mother is a black queen, Ishmael, and that's why I wanted her. You are lucky to have the essence of white and black, and I'm proud of you. From now on, you must promise to tell me what's going on at school. Let me coach you on how to deal with those nasty little pricks. Remember I said I sold out with you? Well, I want to be the coolest dad ever, but I sold out because I felt nurturing your God-given talent was much better for you. There'll be no more of that – you hear me?"

"Yeah, Dad, I hear you."

"Good. Now, go upstairs and wash up. Let's go out for burgers – the higher stacked the better!"

I went upstairs to my room, showered, and looked for some casual clothes. After finding some clean, pressed jeans and a collared shirt, I was about to head downstairs when but I was stopped dead in my tracks.

She was there.

In my bedroom.

I couldn't see her, but I *knew* she was there.

It smelled like Sarah; I felt her presence.

Sitting down on the soft carpet, I felt an invisible force ram into my body, just like my sweet little sister used to do.

Then, just like that, she disappeared.

Part II: Chapter Ten

T hings went back to normal.

Sadly, I think I actually liked it that way. Granted, I hated food being thrown and being called *Pissmael*, but at least it was *my* reality, a reality in which I was fully cognizant. My fellow students were all cocksuckers, but they were *my* cocksuckers, and I could deal with them accordingly.

My resolve to not succumb to bad temptations was still ingrained in me, but even after a few weeks, what I'd done to Mrs. Allen still hadn't even twinged me with guilt. The fat old bat deserved it, and my only regret was not being able to see her in the hospital – I wanted to see her suffer first-hand as she paid for what she'd done and said to me.

One weekend, my father took me back to the Ashford Association of Patriots. Pastor Jadrich Lima had been preaching for a few months, and his congregation was swelling in numbers quickly. The people of Ashford really seemed to associate with his message. Although I knew he caused my family a lot of grief, I was curious to discover what drew so many people toward him.

As we walked into the church, I was amazed to see how many more folks were there since my last time. Every pew was full, and people were chatting among themselves. When we walked in, a handful of people –many of whom I'd never seen before – approached my father and shook his hand. None of them acknowledged my presence until I extended my hand. I wanted to ask Dad why they'd all ignored me, but I was afraid I already knew the answer – I was certain one of the couples were Erin's parents. Word had gotten around I'd made her cry, and no doubt the story as to why had been embellished to make me look terrible and her like a blonde, blameless, innocent angel. Regardless, I wasn't scared of them or the rest of the congregation. I was young and black; nobody would expect anything but the worst from me.

My father and I sat ourselves down on a wooden pew. He didn't go to the dining hall for refreshments, and I felt that was because he didn't want me to be forced to eat in a room that didn't want me there.

As I sat there, I noticed there were no Bibles in the cubby at the back of the pew in front of me. That did seem strange for a supposed church. Others in the congregation seemed confused as well, but that only lasted until Pastor Lima approached the pulpit.

"My brothers and sisters… welcome. I am truly humbled to see how quickly we have grown as a family – from a mere handful to a whole community! Indeed, a higher power has looked down on us with favor – and why not? We are the chosen ones after all.

"First and foremost, I would like to welcome back Mr. Samuel Abias. I doubt any of us could walk an inch in his troubled shoes, yet here he is among us – and he has brought his son so they could see the light together.

"Now, today, I want to take a moment to discuss something near and dear to my heart. The subject of the rights of mankind over others. Unlike some people around the world, we understand we were all created equal before the eyes of God. One man does not have dominion over another man. Now, this we know to be true.

"But… we must consider the fact that equality comes *only* in the eyes of God; we sure ain't born equal, are we? Some of us are born into a life of luxury, and others into poverty. Now, I'm not one to question why the Almighty does such a thing, but I have faith it is all part of *His* ultimate plan.

"All of this should make it obvious that some of us have to work harder than others to reap the same benefits. Take a man born into poverty, for example – he goes without food while someone else's belly is full. Therefore, I ask you all, don't we have a responsibility to help out our fellow brothers and sisters? I would say *yes* because we don't know what the Almighty has planned. Maybe it's all part of His plan to show Satan the resilience of free will?

"I am under the impression this is decreed by the Almighty, but we supposedly live in a society of justice. We may be loving and equal, but we sure as Hell ain't no fools, are we? I warn you all, there will be some of those among us who choose to cheat the system. They don't wish to carry their own weight, and neither did their fathers, and *their* fathers before them. There are those in this world who put their faith in false leaders and then cry *inequality* when the world hasn't bent to their will.

"And, there are those in this world who, although born equal, would not drink from the water when led to it. Think about it: am I to be blamed when a starving fool won't eat the food I give him and meets his maker due to starvation?

"Therefore, my brother and sisters, I want to you to consider one important fact: if shown the light, why would others refuse? Were not the Jews, Muslims, Hindus, and whatever the hell else people believe in on this Earth made aware of the chosen path? Maybe they can't join us, but they can have appreciation for us in their hearts and support our causes... *but they do not.*

"Therefore, I want us to think about what Jesus would do? Well –"

Pastor Lima was cut off by a woman who appeared to work for the Church; she walked up to the pulpit and whispered something in Lima's ear.

"Excuse me. I'll be right back," the preacher said.

My father he put a finger to his lips to tell me to *shush*. Others in the congregation around me looked around and whispered quietly to their neighbors. I reckoned that, by the way Lima was interrupted, everyone though something serious was going on; the tension was palpable.

A few minutes later, Pastor Lima returned, his personable demeanor changed. He looked somber, upset, shocked.

"My dear brothers and sisters, I just received word from Ashford General Hospital. Brenda Allen, a proud, dedicated member of our family who devoted her life to caring for our children at Ashford Elementary, passed away a few hours ago. I'm afraid we must delay our discussion about what Jesus would do for another day. I simply was not expecting this. Let us pray."

The congregation bowed their heads and prayed along with Lima. My dad was not a praying man, so it was awkward to see him with his eyes closed in solemn prayer; I'm sure he was just doing it for appearances.

As for me though, I felt myself begin to convulse; vomit rose up my esophagus. My father opened his eyes and asked if I was okay.

I couldn't answer.

Instead, I threw up. Thankfully, caught most of it in my mouth; only a small squirt of vomit – consisting of eggs and toast – came out splashed onto the floor. Standing up quickly,

I ran to the bathroom. As I ran off, I heard Pastor Lima speaking.

"A young, and tortured soul," he said. "Poor, young Ishmael can't stomach the thought of losing his beloved teacher. His action stands testament to Brenda Allen's kind nature and warmth. If you wish to see her legacy on our children students, look no further than this very church. Bless you, Ishmael, and know that your dear Mrs. Allen is looking down upon you."

Lima's voice trailed off as I got to the restroom. Thank God for that – if I'd had to listen to another second about how the nasty old cow was an inspiration in my life, I think I'd have vomited *and* shit my pants at the same time.

I ran to the sink and threw up.

The chucks of my vomit were too large to fit down the drain, and the sight of it made me puke some more. My stomach was working on a complete evacuation.

My father and a handful men from the congregation ran into the restroom. Dad helped me stay on my feet while the others gave me cups of ice water and bottles of cold water. One brought in a nice, cold Sprite – I was thankful for that as Sprite tastes incredible and stops vomit in its tracks.

"Dad, I'm sorry, I just can't…"

"Not a word, Son. You just go right ahead and do what you need to do. We're going straight home after this."

"You sure?"

"Don't you worry about things *I* need to worry about. Are you alright?"

"Yeah." I cleaned my mouth and face with chill water from the tap. I felt refreshed. As I stepped out into hallway, an older man poured the Sprite into an ice cup and handed to me. I smiled and accepted with gratitude, "Thank you, sir."

"Anytime, Son," he said.

The first touch of the tingly, lemony carbonation recharged my body and gave me renewed vigor. Immediately, I felt better.

"Ready to go?" asked Dad.

"Can I say bye to Pastor Lima?"

My father looked at me. "That won't be necessary," he said quietly.

So, I said bye to the men who had come to my aid and followed Dad out to the car.

Dad didn't say much for most of the trip home. I figured he wanted me to be alone with my thoughts of Mrs. Allen – but, of course, he didn't know what my thoughts *really* were. I wasn't mourning the loss of a beloved teacher at all. On the contrary, a big part of me was *happy* she was gone. But that didn't suggest I couldn't understand the enormity of what I'd done.

I'd *killed* someone.

I stared out of the car's window, lost in deep philosophical thought as the buildings and vehicles cars went by. I hoped maybe, just maybe, Mrs. Allen's death wasn't my fault. Maybe she'd died of something else? If her cause of death was never publicized, I could live comfortably in denial for the rest of my life – I'd never be tempted to look up her death certificate in the Hall of Records. Maybe that could work. As we neared our neighborhood, my father finally spoke.

"Why did you ask to say goodbye to Pastor Lima?" he asked me.

"Huh?"

"Before we left, you asked to say bye to Pastor Lima. Son, I expected you to have more pride than that. You know I was only there because I'm selling out for work, and you also know what he told the congregation to make that little girl try to give us charity."

"I was selling out too, Dad."

"I see." He turned his head away.

As we approached our neighborhood, my father missed the turn. With a huff, he drove to the next entrance to take us to the rear entrance of our house. It meant passing the wooden cross in our neighbor's yard that marked the exact place where Sarah died in my arms.

I felt better.

Whether or not I had anything to do with Brenda Allen's final demise, she was gone. God had spoken, and I was just the vessel to His will.

Part II: Chapter Eleven

Being black and a kid in Ashford, Ohio had its advantages: Nobody expected shit from me and nobody expected a rational thought or gesture that might have any profound impact on their lives. Nah, they just expected me to sound inferior, act inferior, and know my place in a world that evidently wasn't meant for me.

Sitting on my bed, I found myself lost in philosophical thoughts no one would ever expect of me. On my mind: the gift of shame. Shame, for me, felt like a sting worse than that of an angry wasp, which I *have* felt before. Unlike the humble bee, those motherfuckers don't have barbs on their stingers, which means they can sting again and again and again – only fatigue stops them from continuing their punishment.

I was rather proud to feel shame.

Shame kept me from eating with my mouth open and grossing out those around me. Shame kept me from shitting in the middle of the street. Come to think of it, the gift of shame prevents people engaging in so many behaviors that are considered unsavory and against the social order.

However, throughout my life, I've learned there are those who twist that evolutionary trait and fabricate it to suit their own agenda. Take, for example, some unaccomplished, ugly motherfucker. To satisfy his own mediocrity and the fact his wife is quite likely also his sister, he uses shame to make the likes of me feel bad for being a *nigger*. Most of the kids at school force their shame upon me to maintain the social pecking order at my expense. In the case of the deceased Mrs. Allen, she clearly felt shame was ingrained within me, kind of like a perverse birthright, so she always treated me like I had something to be ashamed of.

I admit, I did feel inadequate for a long time – that's why I accepted my place on the broken chair and usually didn't fight back when I got called Pissmael. Worse still, I apologized to Mrs. Allen and Mr. Janicek when they chastised me.

Everyone has a breaking point, and seeing as how I was no Pope, Muhammed, Jesus of Nazareth, or even a Hindu deity – let's pick one; Lakshmi – mine wasn't quite as far off. I was pushed too far one too many times, and that's why Brett lost his shoes and Erin brushed her hair with shit from the boys' toilet.

But then, I was pushed around for the last time, which resulted in a break in my character: I'd been pushed around by *God*.

I watched Sarah die; she closed her eyes in my arms on the side of the street. The last person she ever saw before fading away was me, and I could do nothing to help her. She'd told me her broken and shattered body *hurt*, because she hoped I would give her some comfort – she didn't ask me to fix it.

And then she was gone.

Whose fault was that? Even the school and my parents couldn't claim this one. I'd been pushed around by the hand of God Himself.

That's why Mrs. Allen had to go. She'd used my shame to her advantage for the last time. Honestly speaking, a part of me sympathized – she was ugly and unintelligent… the list went on. Who the fuck would want to be Brenda Allen?

I was just a child. Innocent. My whole future was ahead of me, and Mrs. Allen used me to negate her own miserable life and mediocrity.

Well, fuck that. I was not a bad person, and I'd done nothing wrong. As the solar system formed, didn't countless astral bodies absorb into larger ones before planets and comets found stability? There was no stability with me and Mrs. Allen.

None.

So, I handled it.

I had a reason and hope in continuing my new life as a good person. My beautiful Claire. She showed me light in the darkness, her hands felt soft in a world of broken glass, and she looked beyond my troubled exterior and had me dig a hole in which to keep our secrets. I had a reason. I had hope. I had ambition.

In a world of dirt, I had the only rose that could grow, and the pricking of its thorns – as I would soon find out – felt exquisite.

Part II: Chapter Twelve

B reakfast was good.

There were the homemade biscuits only Mom could make. Dad made the bacon and the eggs as usual. He was no good with the oven.

We sat together as a family and enjoyed our meal. For once, my father didn't talk about grades, and Mom didn't claim any moral superiority. They even asked me about the troubles I was having at school and offered advice on how to deal with it. Even though I was happy to gain their insight, a small spark within me that remembered the way they'd made me feel most of my life ignited. After all, they were an interracial couple living in the United States and had never considered I might be able to learn from their struggle.

It had taken the death of my sister.

"You got something on your mind, Ishmael?" Mom asked once my father finished his breakfast and left for work.

I nodded.

"Is it about that teacher who went off on you? The one who died?"

"Yeah."

"Well, she's gone now, Honey. I know she was a dirt-bag, but I'm sure you still feel *something*."

"I do. Why did she treat me like that? I never knew how to make her stop."

"If you fight very battle that comes to you, you'll fight forever," Mom said. "You can't control the will of others – so there's virtue in letting go. It doesn't make you a wimp. It's degrading to the bullies, because even when they call your mom a *nigger*, they're still not good enough to make you mad. Trust me, they feel that."

"It doesn't work; they never stop and they enjoy treating me like crap."

"I understand, and I'm going to ask you to do something a mother shouldn't have to ask her child. I want you to *bear* it. Just live inside your head. There is hope: I saw your father preparing his resume. He's finally had enough of this God-awful town too, given how he's been treated at work and that horrible church."

"That's good." I gave Mom a smile. "But some seem okay. Mr. Greg isn't rude to him."

"Honey, all of those people hate both him and me. But let me tell you something I want you to remember. You need to be thankful for those who are rude to our faces. They show us their *true* nature everyday so we don't have to wonder about them. The ones to *really* worry about hide behind a mask, and sadly it's often a nice mask. Trust your instincts. Don't be too quick to trust anyone. We'll be out of here soon, baby."

"I hope so, Mom."

"And given the son of a bitch who hit Sarah didn't even bother to stop, I think we know this town will do nothing to help us."

"I suppose so," I said.

"Now off to school with you – just one more day 'til the weekend!"

I grabbed my things and headed off to school – knowing full-well what I was walking into: while some kids were a little kinder to me, Brett and his cohorts had decided to resume their old ways. Treating me like a human being after Sarah died was something I reckoned they all felt they needed to do, and it must have been awkward as fuck for them to do so. Abuse was in their nature; it's what they were taught, and the death of my sister forced their true nature into submission.

I got to school, and to my surprise, no one paid attention to me. Even Brett and his crew were ignoring me. However, they were doing too good a job of it, like they were *intentionally* not noticing me – so much so, I knew they were actually paying more attention to me than anyone. It felt odd, but I remembered what Mom had said about bearing it. As long as they didn't *physically* harm me, I'd be just fine.

I'd continue to live inside my own head.

I went to class and sat at my seat at the back as usual. Mr. Janicek didn't say anything to me and didn't start class at the usual time. It was like he was waiting for something.

The morning announcements started up, which normally didn't start until the beginning of second period:

"Good morning, students. This is Principal Labar. We are going to change things up today and start our day with morning announcements. I don't know if any of you have heard the news about Mrs. Allen. I am very sorry to be the bearer of bad news, but she sadly passed away on Sunday. I know this must be hard for you to hear, and please know the counsellors' office is always open if you need to speak to someone about it.

It's never easy to lose somebody, especially friends and family. When I think of Mrs. Allen, I feel like I have lost family. She devoted her life to all of you at the school. Her only wish in life was to see you all safe and happy.

Unfortunately, heart attacks caused by stress can be very sudden and unexpected, as it was for Mrs. Allen. I hope what happened to her serves as a reminder to us all to always be kind to one another. Nothing in this life is guaranteed, except love from our parents and the grace of God.

Today, I call on each of you to make today the best day ever and show Mrs. Allen what our student body is made of. Show her what she left behind and how wonderful she made our school.

Thank you all, and have a loving weekend.

I couldn't fucking believe it!

The old bat had died of a fucking heart attack!

A big part of me was relieved I wasn't a killer; the potential ramifications of that were starting to catch up to me. But, even knowing I'd broken one of the ten commandments, I felt some resolve for what I'd done. I felt I'd righted the universe in a way, honored Sarah's name, and stood up for myself. Now, even in death, Mrs. Allen mocked me – she hadn't taken care of herself for years, and her old heart had killed her before blood sugar ever could.

She'd robbed me of my liberation.

But that wasn't the only way she'd had the final laugh at my expense: Everyone in my class was in the lunch room that day she'd dragged me away. Principal Labar said stress caused heart attacks and I had a feeling she'd insinuated I was the catalyst. That appeared to resonate with my classmates, and they all seemed to be glancing at me. Brett, Mark, Erin, and some other kids eyed me with a look of disgust.

My resolve to be a better person was short-lived. The torment that was my life had resurrected once more, but things were different: I had the killer instinct within me.

That day during lunch, I sat in my broken desk but did not eat anything. I didn't wish to appear vulnerable. I sat and stared off into space, focusing on nothing in particular.

Part II: Chapter Thirteen

That Sunday, my father took me to the Ashford Associations of Patriots Church. As usual, he was reluctant to go, and being the man he was, he wasn't able to compartmentalize his emotions. So, naturally, I kept quiet in the car. I was prepared to discuss my schoolwork and give him a convincing speech about an undying commitment to my education should he decide to speak – anything to keep him off my back.

Luckily, he didn't say a word.

As for me, I wasn't in the worst of moods. Ever since Principal Labar's announcement about Mrs. Allen's demise, I feared what might be in store for me next at school, but the week went by without incident. I still sat alone during lunch at my broken desk. I still didn't eat and was pretty damn hungry by the time I got home, but I was careful not to do anything to disrupt the status quo.

My dad reached the intersection right before Lima's church. He didn't make the yellow light before it turned red and had to slam his brakes.

"Asshole!" He thumped steering wheel. Given he didn't even want to go to the church, I thought it strange he was mad about being a few minutes late.

Once at the church, we parked and made our way through the church's front door. The congregation was *huge*, and we'd made it in time – the sermon hadn't even begun. I saw the same familiar faces milling around, and even some of the kids from school.

"Let's not worry about socializing, Ishmael," Dad said to me and pointed at an empty space on a nearby pew. "Just sit with me and look like you're reading and in prayer. They won't question why we aren't talking to anyone if we do that. Grab a Bible."

"I don't think there are any Bibles – remember?"

"Shit," Dad grumbled, his voice a whisper. "You're right. Okay, just sit next to me and lower your head in prayer."

"We don't pray…" I protested.

"Damn it, Ishmael! I know that!" Dad's face reddened. "Just *look* like you are. Can't you just shut up and help me out here?" He spoke loud enough for anyone within earshot to hear his desperation, a thunderous whisper. Strangely, it felt comfortable to hear him sound like his usual self.

So, we sat together on the pew and clasped our hands together as if in silent prayer. I got to thinking about the nurse in the hospital with the gorgeous body. Yeah, I was in place of worship, but it's so easy for the mind to get distracted into thinking about things we aren't supposed to.

My pleasant reverie didn't last long.

From outside came familiar sounds: Dribbling. I didn't even know the Church had a basketball court. I thought about asking Dad if I could maybe go out and play, but reality slapped me back to my senses. Who would I see there? Friends? Claire? Dismissing my foolish thoughts, I stayed silent and pretended to pray silently.

But then the worst thing ever happened.

"Ishmael, maybe you should go outside and mingle with the other kids – make some friends," Dad whispered.

"I don't have friends, Dad. They won't want me."

"Don't give me the same bullshit everywhere we go," my father snapped. "This is a church, not school. Kids are nice here."

"It's the same kids," I protested. "Being here won't change them."

"Ishmael." Dad's voice a reverent whisper. "Go outside and introduce yourself. People aren't mean and don't tease others at church. But, if they do, just tell them it's church and they need to be decent!"

There was no point arguing with Dad once his mind was made up.

Standing up, I made my way over to the side door. I took a deep breath, braced myself, and opened the door.

Once outside, I saw the basketball court. Head down, prepared to be shunned, I walked over.

Approaching the court, I realized only one person was playing – a girl. However awkward I thought the situation might be, it was magnified a thousand-fold. Being shunned by boys would be embarrassing enough once it got back to school, but being kicked off the court by a girl would so much worse.

Damn my father! I vehemently told him I didn't want to go outside.

"Ishmael?"

Looking up, I couldn't believe my eyes. "Claire!"

"Hi!"

"I didn't know you liked basketball!"

"My step-mom told me to come out here. Pastor Lima gave me the basketball. My parents are just trying this place out because it seems like *everybody* comes here now."

"My dad and me have been coming for a while now," I told her.

Claire took a shot and missed.

I picked up the ball and took a shot myself; nothing but net.

"Do you like it?"

"No," I admitted. "It seems to upset my family a lot. They say a lot of things here that hurts people like us. Sometimes my dad comes alone – and he's always angry when he comes back."

"How so?"

"You can't tell anyone, Claire – promise?" It was the first time I'd asked anything of her. In a way, I felt like it bonded us even more.

"I promise!"

"Remember in the school library when we talked about me being half-black?"

"Uh huh." Claire nodded. She took another shot and missed. The basketball bounced on the pavement. When it came to a stop, I picked it up and held it in my arms.

"I think Lima said something because when my dad's work people thought he wasn't there, he caught them praying and saying God was angry at him for marrying a Black woman and making me." I took another shot; the ball bounced on the metal rim and fell off the side. Claire didn't go for the rebound. She moved her hair away from her pretty face and tucked it behind her ear before looking right at me. I noticed she wore pink, dangly earrings.

"What?"

"Yeah, and they gave my family five thousand dollars to pay for my sister's funeral."

"Why do that if your dad did such a bad thing?"

"I really don't know. He was *really* mad about it."

Claire walked up to me, right as I was about to take a shot, and took the basketball away from me. She dropped it to the ground. It bounced a few times and landed in the grass. The sun shone upon her face, her beautiful, flawless white skin glowing in its warm light; her blonde hair wafted in the soft breeze. Claire took my hands in hers and held them gently.

"I feel so bad that I can't stand up for you," she said. "But I do know God loves you, Ishmael. I wish my dad wasn't so mean and racist, but he is – so I can't say anything to help."

"I know, Claire, you already told me, and I never forgot. It doesn't hurt my feelings when you don't say anything to defend me."

A single tear formed in the corner of Claire's eye.

"Claire?" I was concerned I'd upset her somehow.

"Sorry…"

"Don't be sorry. I'll be fine as long as you're my friend."

"I feel like you're the only one who *really* understands me," Claire sobbed.

"What do you mean?"

"I promised I'd keep your secret, Ishmael, can you keep mine?"

"Of course." The tear fell from Claire's eye and ran down her cheek. Freeing a hand, I used its side to brush the tear away. Claire blushed and looked away – but not out of discomfort.

"Okay." She released my other hand and put her hands on the bottom of her shirt. Then, she lifted it halfway up her stomach, and what I saw would haunt me for the rest of my life: a ragged, red scar on her sides, an inch or two above her hips. Turning slightly, Claire let me see that the scar went all the way round to her back.

"What's that?" My voice choked but I somehow managed to get the words out.

"My family hits me," Claire said, speaking softly. "My brother said he would come back for me one day, but he hasn't. Neither has Sanjana. I guess they don't love me. I wanted to show you because I think your parents hit you."

"Why would you think that?" I asked as Claire lowered her shirt.

"I can tell by looking at you, Ishmael," Claire told me. "Kids like us just *know*, I think. I don't know for certain – is it true. Do they?"

I took a deep breath. "Yes," I said with my head down.

"One day, Ishmael, one day, we will be free. Then I will be there for you. I can be your friend and I can…" Claire's face froze as she looked into the distance behind me.

"Claire?"

She looked nervous, *desperate*.

"Ishmael, you have to come with me," Claire urged. "Don't turn around. Just come with me – quickly!" She took my hand again and led me away toward a large electric company box on the grass verge. We both sat down behind the box; Claire held a finger up to her lips. She looked pretty when she did that, but I had no time to admire her. Panicking, I had no idea what the hell was going on.

Seconds later, I heard footsteps and indiscernible voices approaching us. The basketball was being bounced, and soon the voice became clearer. Claire grabbed my hand and held it tightly. Thank God they couldn't see us.

"We alone?" said one of the voices.

"Yeah, we're all good."

They sounded familiar: I knew them from school.

"Erin coming?"

"She said she might. I don't know if she didn't come to church or if she couldn't come outside."

"I saw her inside. She coming out?"

"I didn't see her. She's probably not allowed then."

"*Sheeeeit.*"

"It's all good. We can talk without her."

"Cool. So, it seems like everyone is playing along *real* good."

Claire kept her head down, determined to not get caught, and it made my resolve stronger. I still couldn't figure out who the voices were, but I figured it'd come to me soon enough.

"Yeah, that fucking nigger doesn't know shit," the first voice said. "I heard Jim and Sean talking shit in the hallway, but I told them to cut it out. Pissmael didn't figure it out, though. Dumb nigger probably thinks everyone is his friend since his little bitch sister died."

"Fuck that little bitch," the other voice snarled. "I wish she'd come back to life so someone could do it again."

"Like a *zombie* nigger?"

As they both laughed, I realized the voices belonged to Brett and Mark. My fists clenched in rage. In my heart, I knew if I stepped out from behind that electric box, I'd have been able to kill them both with a clear conscience. Claire felt my tension and held my hand tighter; she looked at me, her lips pouty and eyebrows raised – she wanted me to stay put.

"So… this Friday?" Mark said.

"Yeah, this Friday," Brett replied with menace. "I'll meet you on the corner at 1:00 a.m. Dad'll be so fucking drunk he'll not know I snuck out. I got the eggs – and you bring the paint. We gonna fuck the nigger house up real good. If you can bring a knife, we'll get his parents' fucking tires too. I can't believe my parents gave a hundred dollars to Erin's family just for Pissmael to be an asshole about it."

"A hundred bucks? My family gave five hundred bucks a few weekends ago to his dad's work. My mom works at the same place. No clue what they did with it! Probably just out having fun!"

"Yeah," Brett said as the basketball bounced rhythmically on the blacktop.

"You *sure* no one knows?"

"Just us and Erin," Brett's voice lowered, but I could still hear him. "She's pretending to feel bad for him and everyone sees her being nice. Dumb nigger. People always listen to cute chicks."

"Yeah, man!" said Mark. "Because they have *tits*!"

The two laughed heartily at Mark's crude comment.

An announcement blaring over the church's loudspeaker interrupted the merriment and made Claire and I jump a little.

The sermon commencing in three minutes! Please make your way back inside.

Staying put, I heard Brett and Mark's voices fade away as they made their way to the church. When Claire and me knew the coast was clear, we emerged from our hiding place.

"Ishmael, what should we do?" Claire's pretty face was a picture of concern.

I had no idea, but I knew I was going to make things right. Brett and Mark had done me a favor by celebrating Sarah's death and calling me a nigger and her a bitch. Silently, I thanked them for that. Those words were fuel to the fire of my anger, and while I didn't know *what* I was going to do, I knew I was going to do *something*.

"I'll make it right, Claire."

"I get hit all the time, Ishmael," Claire said quietly. "Even when I'm good, my parents hit me. So, if I'm bad, I'll be hit just the same. I want to help you with whatever you decide to do. I want to hang out with you at school, too."

While I had no plan, my gut told me it was important to maintain the status quo; it would help.

"Not right now," I told Claire. "Let's keep things the same. Ignore me for now, but you'll know when it's time to help me."

"Ishmael –" Claire began.

I lifted my hand and placed a finger against her soft lips; it was her turn to be shushed. "Please trust me, Claire," I said and nodded toward Lima's church. "You go first – I'll give it a few minutes before I come in."

Holding my hand, Claire pushed my finger away from her lips, leaned forward, and kissed me on the lips. My knees wobbled, and I almost fell; thank God I didn't. Then, she then turned around and ran back to the church.

I went back inside two minutes later and sat next to my dad, just as Pastor Lima began his sermon.

Part II: Chapter Fourteen

"I am so glad to see Samuel Abias here with us today. And his strong son, Ishmael. If y'all wouldn't mind, would you two stand up?"

Dad nudged me with his elbow and we stood up. Some of the congregation looked at us with love and sympathy, others with disgust.

"I wanted y'all two to stand up so we could witness what suffering for the Lord looks like – right here before us in the flesh! I also want the congregation to see where our kind, selfless acts of charity and sacrifice lead. You can see for yourself the faces of the ones you helped save. For, when the Lord blesses you, you should always give some back – and give back, y'all did now! Y'all two can be seated.

"Now, I just want you two to know that you aren't to be judged for anything that may have happened in the past, and I sure hope nobody here today does that or assumes I'm referring to any particular sin. We are all sinners and pay in our own way. The lord is truly mysterious, is He not?

"And, as the Abiases will tell you, it is important for us to trust in the Lord and know that everything – as painful and wrong as it may seem – is His work. Even something as terrible as losing a loved one is insignificant when viewed as part of God's master plan. We must accept. We must accept with no question, and accept all His decisions. And, if there is something to learn, we'd best learn it and learn it quick, for every day we are alive after a tragedy is another chance for us to get with God's good graces.

"And, speaking of loss, I want to bring up a loss we all felt recently: Brenda Allen. Now, I am not the Lord, and never do I claim such a title, but one cross we bear is our reputation – and let me tell you, you can put hers where the sun definitely do shine. Brenda was a true patriot. She was a proud, submissive wife, and she loved nothing more than God, her country, and the school children in her care. She lived to serve those children.

"Now, considering God may have us suffer a tragedy to right a wrong, why would He take such a patriot from us?

"Well, He spoke to me, and I can answer a question as confusing as horse doing a jiggy. God needed Brenda Allen for Himself. You heard me right. She was better off in Heaven than down here with sinners and those who caused her stress after she was ordained to right a grave wrong against charity. Oh yes. And I hope her death is a constant reminder of what we can lose if we don't change our ways. To my people, my flock, I say stay truthful, stay loyal, and stay patriotic. Dismissed."

Part II: Chapter Fifteen

L ima's audacity was not to be reckoned with.

He'd basically said Sarah's death was tragic yet justified because it was will of the Lord. Many would subscribe to that, but it's the silent part that isn't to be spoken out loud. And he'd said it right there in front of my dad and me with no fear at all. At the same time, he'd attributed Mrs. Allen's death to some beautiful divine intervention. I was as pissed off as my dad.

I had no time to dwell upon it, however. Claire and I had heard what Brett, Mark, and Erin were planning; I had to get through this week and think of something by then.

Luckily, I'd also overheard about Erin playing nice to get my guard down. I was glad I'd heard it because it gave me clarity.

It helped me focus.

The entire week went off with no issues. Mr. Janicek treated me the same as the other kids – he even called on me a few times to answer questions and praised me when I answered correctly. Of course, I knew he was not part of Erin's nefarious plan – that would be crossing a boundary – so I had no idea what caused him to change his attitude toward me. Had he finally begun to see me a human being?

Did he repent and change his ways? Well, whatever the reason, it made for a welcome change.

On Tuesday, I walked into the lunchroom and felt my life had changed forever. I couldn't believe what I saw; tears welled up in my eyes.

The broken table was gone.

My one sanctuary from the horrible excuse for a school was no longer there. All that remained was an empty corner of dust and debris where it used to be.

I started to panic, but then reminded myself I'd not bought my food. I couldn't begin to imagine the humiliation I'd have felt with a full lunch tray in my hands and struggling to find someplace to sit. I hadn't eaten in the lunchroom in a few weeks – and that habit finally paid off.

I didn't know what to do.

My body was walking into the lunchroom while my mind was walking out. Acting upon instinct, I found myself leaving – but with no plan as to where to go.

I decided to approach Principal Labar to ask if I could have lunch in the library. He'd allowed it once, and I was sure he'd let me do it again. If the principal didn't understand or sympathize with me having nowhere to sit, at least I knew my mother would appreciate my resistance to obey. According to Mom, my father was coming around, and perhaps it would be my time to witness that.

Turning around, I stepped back into the hallway. My resolve was suddenly strong; I felt I would be able to tell Principal Labar anything and stand my ground if I needed to. I would tell him about what Mrs. Allen had done to me every single day. I would tell him about my initial experience with Mr. Janicek. I would tell him all the things Erin, Brett, Mark, and the rest of the kids did to torment me. What was the worst that could happen? Principal Labar didn't believe me and would call my parents so I'd get a massive ass-kicking when I got home?

It was just a short stroll down the hallway.

A firm hand landed on my shoulder. I looked around and saw Mr. Gracen.

"Hello, Ishmael. How's everything going for you today?"

"Hi, I'm doing good." The hesitation was clear in my tone.

"Where ya headin' off to now, *mah* boy?"

"Umm, just going to ask the office a question. Nothing in particular," I responded.

"Now, Son, I know you're *fibbin'*. You feel like there is no place to sit in that there lunch room, huh?"

I shook my head as resolutely as I could.

"I've been watching you, and no smart young man like you should be sittin' in the corner like that."

"I'm fine with it. I actually like to sit there."

"Now, Son," Mr. Gracen said in a way I figured was meant to be reassuring, "I've been around a long time, and I sees a young man who won't sit with other kids because he's too scared. That's why I had the janitor take that there broken desk away. Heck, it's not even safe with all them splinters and rough edges."

I was furious – betrayed and stabbed in the back by none other than my own kind.

"Please, I said I don't want to go back in there!" My voice rose. I felt bad for raising my voice to Mr. Gracen; he meant no harm. But my desperation was more pressing than my manners.

"No, Son, I can't stand by and see *yuh* like this here," Mr. Gracen insisted. He leaned toward me so no one else could hear him. "Men like *us* don't get respect, so we have to *demand* it. You know what I mean, Son?"

"But…" My resistance was futile.

With a firm hand on my shoulder, Mr. Gracen gently ushered me back into the lunchroom and looked around. At the church, I'd begged Claire to keep our relationship to herself, but I really hoped she'd break her promise to me. I usually saw her during lunch sitting over in the corner with popular kids. That day, I didn't see her anywhere.

Mr. Gracen soon noticed an empty seat – by none other than Erin, Brett, and Mark, who sat at the same table. It made sense the three would be together.

As we approached the table, I felt nervous even though I was internally confident – I knew what those fuckers were planning. Erin was nibbling at a pink cupcake, Brett ate a hot dog and chips, and Mark was chewing on a slice of dry school pizza that resembled tomato sauce and cheese on a square of drywall.

Erin looked so pretty; I felt like shit for noticing.

"Hello, kids," Mr. Gracen said with a wide, toothy smile. "Seems like Ishmael here has no place to sit. How about this empty chair? Y'all have room for a new friend?"

The man certainly wasn't subtle – or quiet – and all the kids close by turned their heads to see what was going on. It was hellishly embarrassing, yes, but I kept on reminding myself I knew what the terrible three had planned for my family.

I had the upper hand.

"Yeah, that's fine!" Erin's voice was most convincing. The bitch was a great actress.

"Okay, then take a seat with your new friends, Ishmael!" Mr. Gracen commanded. As I sat down, he flashed me a warm smile and walked away. The guy looked like he felt he'd accomplished something that day that would change a child's life.

"Hey, guys," I mumbled, refusing to look at any of the three. "Sorry, I was trying go to the library but he stopped me."

"It's okay, Ishmael," Erin said. "You don't want to sit with us?" She actually managed to look offended.

"I do. But I thought you were mad at me for, ya know, the money thing."

"That's okay. It *was* a lot of money, and you can take it later if you want."

"Thanks." I felt like I was losing the upper hand. Nothing seemed backhanded on Erin's part – she was keeping things ostensibly genuine.

"You're the kid who likes Star Wars?" Mark chipped in. He looked right at me, paying me too much attention, and sounding unnatural; the fucking rat couldn't act to save his life. All he did was reaffirm he and his two cohorts did indeed have a conspiracy against me.

"Yeah, they're my favorite movies ever," I responded.

"Which one is your total favorite, man?"

"Return of the Jedi," I told Mark.

"Hell yeah! *I am your father!*"

I didn't correct him.

***

That evening, I had dinner early and started on my homework right away. I wasn't normally so keen, as I could finish it without the fabricated urgency my father considered necessary, but I needed to keep things at home in order.

The whole week continued along the same lines.

The only deviation from the normal happened on Wednesday. I was sitting quietly with Erin, Mark, and Brett, when she looked straight at me. Twirling a strand of hair in her finger, she asked me, "So, Ishmael, what are you doing this weekend? Watching Star Wars?"

"No," I said. "I've seen it so many times."

"Yeah. I get that. What about Friday? Just hanging out at home?"

Real subtle, bitch.

"Actually, I'm going out of town with my folks," I lied. "We're back Saturday morning."

"Oh, really?" There was a distinct sparkle in the scheming bitch's eyes.

"Yeah – we're going to Ohio State to visit my cousin."

"Fun!" Erin declared with a pretty smile spreading across her face.

That was the first day I decided to eat during lunch – I felt it important to keep up the façade of falling into submission, being sucked in by their play-acting. As I looked down at my burger, in my peripheral vision, I saw Erin looking meaningfully at Brett and Mark.

Besides Erin, everyone else at school who was part of the conspiracy to be nice to me exposed what poor thespians they really were. They either looked away from me too intentionally or made a big spectacle to be kind.

Idiots.

On Thursday morning, things felt strange.

I woke up, climbed out of my bed and, as I stepped into the shower, I noticed my feet felt *slimy* as warm water ran over them. Looking down, I saw brown water was rinsing away from the bottom of my soles. I lifted a foot, but it was already clean; I had no idea what to make of it.

Turning the water to hot, I felt a sharp sting on my ankles. Upon further scrutiny, I discovered tiny scrapes in my skin. My nose and throat also felt stuffy, yet my lips felt incredibly soft with the taste of strawberry saliva in my mouth – it was as if I'd been kissed by an angel.

Part II: Chapter Sixteen

That Friday, I went to school limping. I didn't suspect there was any damage to my ankle, but enough skin had been scraped off to make walking a little uncomfortable.

School was just like any other day, but more kids than usual were looking at me, and countless times I'd happen upon someone talking to Brett or Mark in the hallway – they'd quickly try to be more discreet and change the subject.

That night was the night.

Those fuckers were going to vandalize my house and destroy my parent's property because they thought we'd be out of town.

That night at the dinner table, I tried to appear as normal as possible. I updated my parents on my schoolwork and talked with enthusiasm about my future career ambitions. I chose *doctor*, but was scolded for not having decided what medical school I intended to apply to.

Home sweet home.

After we'd finished eating and I was clearing the table, Dad stood up and poured himself a beer. "Mad, are you coming to bed?"

"I'm not tired," Mom replied. "I'll catch some TV and try to fall asleep."

"I need my mind to relax a little bit before tomorrow," Dad said. "I'll stay up with you."

Fuck.

They were usually in bed by 9:00 p.m. every night, with lights out at 10:00 p.m. I hoped to all holy Hell the change of habit not delay them too much – it was already 7:00 p.m.

Running upstairs, I looked out onto the street. Nothing so far. The street was still, devoid of life – there was one flickering street light, which gave a little movement to the dark road ahead. My heart felt so damn heavy: a little way beyond that was where my sweet little sister passed away in my arms and became my angel.

By contrast, that night, I was on the lookout for demons.

I watched over the next hour, but nobody came. A few cars passed by, but no one on foot. Not one single soul. I knew Brett and Mark had agreed upon 1:00 a.m., but I reckoned they'd already be casing the house, watching us like wild predators cloaked in darkness. I wondered that if they saw Dad's car in the driveway, they'd realize I'd lied about us going out of town – but then I reminded myself neither Brett, Mark, nor Erin knew how many cars we actually had.

Brett had said his dad had to be drunk before he could sneak out, and it was still early. Time was still on my side.

It was 8:30 p.m., and my parents would be in bed before long. While I still had no plan, I knew the time would come when I'd have to act. I had faith I'd know what to do by then. Sarah was watching over me, and for once, my commitment to justice was not solely with Claire: my sister died just across that road.

I went downstairs under the guise of needing a glass of water, and found my parents still there. They were watching some movie based on a Stephen King novel. I didn't know which one, but it wasn't scary – so the movie probably wasn't close to being done.

Dammit!

"Ishmael? Everything okay?" Mom spotted me.

"Just thirsty," I told her, and she went back to the movie.

In the fridge, there was unopened can of soda. I wasn't allowed soda before bed, and I did know from experience that three things would happen if I opened it: my parents would hear the satisfying crack and fizz, I would be told I can't have soda, and they'd tell me to pour it out for them.

That's when I had the idea.

My mother could never sleep properly after Sarah died and relied heavily on sleeping pills. They were in the nightstand on her side of her bed.

I took the soda can and opened it so they would hear the noise.

"Ishmael, do you have problems with your memory?" Dad called over.

"No."

"Then tell me in plain English why you are having soda at this time of the night?"

"I forgot. Sorry."

"If you need me to write it in other languages or draw you a picture, then please say so. Put it down."

"Okay. Sorry."

"Actually, you can pour two glasses – for me and Mom." There was no politeness in his tone, as usual.

"Yes, Dad," I said. "I'll be right back."

"Ishmael?" my mom called after me as I ran up the stairs. Quietly, I snuck into my parent's bedroom, opened the nightstand drawer, and grabbed two sleeping pills. I then stomped into the bathroom with heavy footsteps so they'd hear me in there. I counted to ten before heading back downstairs with Mom's pills safely in my pocket.

"Ishmael? Where did you go?" asked Mom.

"I had to fart really bad, and it would be rude to do it here," I told her, looking as embarrassed as possible.

"Can't blame the boy, Mad!" Dad chuckled. "Ishmael can clear a room with one of his farts!"

As Mom joined in with his laughter, I took the soda can from the countertop and two glasses from the cabinet. I retrieved the pills from my pocket and opened the tiny capsules. Then, I poured the contents of each one into the glasses and poured the fizzy drink on top; lucky for me, the fine powder dissolved instantly.

I took the drinks to my parents and they gulped them down – suspecting nothing.

Back in my room, I continued staring out of the window. Sitting there in my pajamas looking over the desolate street, I felt scared. I'd just drugged my parents. But the adrenaline rush of that had worn down and the gravity of what I'd done hit me. Why didn't I just tell my parents what I'd overheard at the church basketball court? What's the worst that could have happened? Why did I feel the need to react the way I had and attempt to take matters into my own hands?

Adrenaline and poor impulse control were my worst enemies and they lived within me; I was my own worst enemy. If only I'd continued dwelling within the atmosphere of my own world, I wouldn't be in that predicament: My parents wouldn't have been drugged by their own son, and the police would be talking to Erin, Mark, and Brett.

Twenty minutes later, I heard my parents making their weary way upstairs. They went into their bedroom and shut the door. I was sure Mom was probably used to the pills, but my dad wasn't – he'd be knocked out first.

But then something hit me: my mother took sleeping pills every night and obviously didn't know I'd already slipped her one. She'd take another. Would that overdose her?

Sitting against my window, a cold terror crept through me: I might have just killed my mom. I truly began to hate myself because I was not totally convinced Brett and Mark were on their way – their plan may just have been big talk between nefarious friends.

Thinking about Sarah, I decided I could sell myself out again. I was built for abuse, and I could easily handle more. Standing up, I prepared to go wake up my parents and confess all.

I took a stretch, and just as I as leaving the window, I saw two dark shapes far in distance. They were short. Not adults, for sure.

Staying low, I watched them walk up the street. They didn't appear confident – each step was with caution, and they kept scoping the road and sidewalks. The two had no flashlights and walked close together.

Three houses away, they stopped and looked up at mine, and I saw their faces.

Brett and Mark.

I looked directly at them, but they didn't see me against the blackness of my room. I wondered if they somehow *sensed* they were being watched.

They carried nothing in their hands. I knew it was just their initial reconnaissance; I pictured Brett's loutish father stinking drunk and passed out on the couch – I had no idea about Mark's family, but nothing would have surprised me about them.

None of that mattered – because Mark and Brett were there.

Just a few minutes later, they walked away. I knew they'd be back. They wouldn't have gone that far only to not go through with what they had planned.

My thoughts darted back to Mom, and I decided the potential harm to our home was far worse than the possibility of the reaction of the extra sleeping pill – surely it would take more than two to overdose?

I thought of what I should do if – *when* – Brett and Mark returned. I had no plan, but they sure as hell did.

Should I attack?

Maybe grab a knife and scare them.

They hadn't said they were bringing weapons – except maybe a knife for Dad's tires – it would just be eggs and paint.

I *could* sneak downstairs and call the police. But the police always know the number that's calling. Unless I waited for Brett and Mark to attack and *then* call; I could then honestly say I saw them from my window.

Actually, that wasn't a bad idea.

Midnight drew close. Showtime was in an hour.

It *really* wasn't a bad idea.

Feeling relieved that I'd decided upon the best course of action, I saw something move a little way down the street, coming from the direction of where Sarah died.

A female.

Her shape was beautiful. She walked with hesitant grace, as if scared of being alone. A lonely damsel in distress. Beneath the street light, I saw the outline of delicate wings stemming from her tiny, thin shoulders.

Was it my Sarah?

Part II: Chapter Seventeen

The small, angelic figure walked slowly down the street.

I couldn't see her face but I knew it was Sarah – back from Heaven to be with me. A tang of guilt pricked my neck – I knew why she was there. I'd settled on calling the police once Brett and Mark made their move, but Sarah *knew* my thoughts. She knew I'd considered confronting them with a knife and, judging by what I'd done to Mrs. Allen, Sarah understood what I was capable of.

It was my first visit from my little sister, and she was upset with me. After she passed, my heart broke – but I accepted my loss as I knew I'd see my sweet Sarah again.

I missed her so much.

She stopped in front of the house, refusing to move further. I waved my hand, beckoning for her to fly up to my window. Sarah didn't move.

I closed my eyes and spoke to her with my mind.

"Sarah, my little monkey. Can't you fly up to see me?"

The small figure outside just stood there.

"Monkey, this is Iss. Come to my room," I thought-said with conviction. I willed my thoughts into her mind, but Sarah remained motionless and just stared. Even though my

room looked black and lifeless from outside, I knew she was looking directly at me, into my very heart and soul.

I rapped my hands three times on the window. It was loud enough for her to hear me, but quiet enough be discreet and not disturb my sleeping parents.

She didn't respond – her gaze was still upon me.

Realizing the futility of my efforts, I crept downstairs. I glanced through the window by the front door and saw Sarah. She was still looking at my bedroom window.

As quietly as I could, I unlocked the door. I opened it silently and peered outside. Sarah saw me and beckoned for me to join her. Normally, I'd have never done such a thing, but I wanted to hold my little sister again.

I closed the door behind me and made my way slowly toward her. When I crossed the street to the opposite sidewalk, she walked toward me.

She stopped beneath a streetlight, her face finally visible on the flickering yellow light.

"Claire?" My breath felt punched from my body.

"Ishmael," my beautiful Claire said with a smile. "How could I not be with you when I know those nasty boys are on their way? I... I... I *love* you, Ishmael. I want to be your girlfriend and marry you when we grow up. Nobody loves me. My parents, my brother, not even Sanjana. No one loves me. But you understand me, and –"

I put my finger to her lips. "You shouldn't be out so late at night. It's dangerous, Claire!" I looked deep into her eyes and took hold of her soft, small hands.

"If something ever happened to you, I'd never feel safe again. So, I came to be with you."

"Claire…"

"There's no time, Ishmael. Brett and Mark will be back soon to do what they have planned to your home. I want to help you."

I fully intended to talk Claire out of it, but saw her eyes were no longer fixed on me. She was staring over my shoulder and down the street.

Suddenly, Claire's grip on my hand tightened and she set off running, pulling me along to the dark shadows in between two houses.

"Claire?" I whispered.

"I saw them," she gasped. "They're still far away – but they're on the way back!" Claire kept her voice hushed.

We squatted low behind a thick bush and watched my house through a gap in the leaves. What felt like an age later, Brett and Mark appeared. They carried a gallon can of paint each and a Kroger shopping bag – most likely filled with eggs.

Moving with surprising stealth, making no sound at all, Brett and Mark put the bag and cans down between my dad's car and our garage. They didn't begin their attack straight away. Instead, they walked around, nonchalantly casing my house.

"They think my family is out of town," I whispered to Claire.

"You told them that?"

"I told Erin. They've been nice to me during lunch, but I know it's all fake."

"Yeah, I know," Claire whispered. "I heard lots of kids planned to be nice to you so Brett and Mark could get you."

"You *knew*?" I was astounded. "Why didn't you tell me at the church?"

"I found out *after*, Ishmael," Claire turned her eyes away, as if ashamed with herself. "I would have told you if I could have." She pointed at my house.

Brett and Mark were back in my driveway, hidden behind the car; they were opening the paint cans with what appeared to be screwdrivers.

It was time.

"What are you going to do, Ishmael?"

"I don't know!" I said a little too loudly. I had no plan, as calling the cops was out of the question the moment I'd ventured outdoors.

A faint but clear voice from my driveway said, *"What the fuck was that?"* And that's when Brett and Mark turned in unison to look directly toward where Claire and me were hiding.

"There's someone over there!" Mark said. Putting down their screwdrivers, they looked like they were preparing to abandon their attack and run; they didn't know *who* might be watching them, and thus couldn't ascertain the threat.

There was no motherfucking way I was going to allow those fuckers to run off and claim they had no bad intentions toward me and my family.

I stood up, ready to defend my home.

Claire kept hold of my hand and said quietly, "Our secrets, Ishmael. Remember where we said we would keep our secrets?"

Leaning over, I kissed her soft lips, and slowly let go of her hand.

Then, without thinking, I ran at Brett and Mark.

"Holy Fuck!" Mark hissed. *"It's the nigger!"*

"You want a nigger, you fucking got one!" I yelled back, not caring if the neighbors might hear.

"You gonna fight us, *Pissmael*?" Brett growled, his fists clenched.

"You pussies would like a two on one fight," I growled. "Nah... I'm gonna stab your parents to death!"

I then hightailed it down the street.

Those two inbred idiots believed me! Even though they couldn't see a knife or a weapon of any sorts in my hand, they actually believed I was on my way to murder their families!

Brett and Mark gave chase, but I had a good head start. Eight houses down, I reached the edge of the woods and ran through the tree line and into the pitch black within. Undeterred by the darkness, I somehow knew my way around, as if by pure instinct; I found I was better able to navigate with my eyes closed.

About one hundred feet into the woods, I reached the hole Claire and I had dug to hide our secrets. The hole didn't seem as deep as I remembered it – most likely the rain had washed in dirt and leaves. Nonetheless, it was still impressively deep.

I squatted behind the large oak tree in complete silence; I was hyper-aware of every noise around me – even the barely audible scurrying of small animals.

Then came the unmistakable sound of human footsteps. Brett and Mark had the advantage of wearing shoes – driven by rush of adrenaline, I'd left the house barefoot. I guessed my feet would surely be bleeding, but that didn't deter me at all.

The footsteps grew closer. I heard Brett and Mark's hushed voices but couldn't make out any actual words.

I remained in complete silence.

When my pursuers were about twenty feet away, one of them suddenly changed course and moved off to the left; I knew everything would have been in vain if I avoided my planned confrontation – they weren't going to get away with it. I felt around on the ground for something hard to throw – maybe a rock or stick – to distract Brett and Mark from my whereabouts.

My fingertips touched something hard and cold – metal. It was the shovel Claire and I had used to dig our Hole of Secrets. The thing was half-buried in dirt and rotting leaves, but it was still where we'd left it.

It felt like a gift from God.

I wriggled the shovel back and forth slowly to get it out of the ground without making a noise. The earth didn't offer much resistance, but Brett and Mark were loud and the sticks snapped loudly with their heavy footsteps. As I worked the shovel out of the ground, inch by inch, my need for stealth was rudely negated.

"There you are, you fucking little nigger." A whispered voice came from above me.

I grabbed that shovel and swung it upwards as hard as I could. I heard – *felt* – the crack of metal hitting bone; then came the soft, heavy *thump* of a body hitting the ground next to me.

Standing up, I looked down. All I could make out in the gloom was the silhouette of a body on the forest floor. I couldn't tell if I'd hit Brett or Mark, as all the body could do was writhe and gurgle. Suddenly, his hand shot out grab my ankle…

Shovel still in my hand, I rammed it down onto his pale wrist. The metal edge sliced deep into my assailant's flesh and bone, cutting through tendons, veins, and arteries alike. I left it there, not wanting him to bleed out. He tried to scream out his pain, but the cries were muffled and gurgling – I'd smashed his jaw up well, and his mouth was filled with blood. I reckoned he wouldn't have much time left before he bled out or drowned in his own fluids.

"You showed me no mercy, you fucking asshole," I snarled. "You tried to fool me at school, but I *knew* what you were all up to." I felt my way down his body with my hands until I found what I was searching for.

"I heard you on the church basketball court," I whispered. The kid's shorts were loose, which made grabbing his testicles much easier. "We heard *everything*. Me and Claire."

My hands squeezed those warm, hairless balls as hard as they could. I felt one of them *give* against my fingers and he let out a shrill, gurgling scream and convulsed in pain; he begged for mercy, his words choked and unintelligible. It would have been nice to feel the superiority of allowing him mercy, but given what he had planned for my home and his cruel, nasty words about Sarah's demise, there would be none.

Balling my fist, I pressed slowly down on his balls with all my strength and weight.

My fallen assailant's strangled, guttural scream was like music to my ears.

As I pulled the shovel from my tormentor's wrist and lifted it high, prepared to hurt him some more, the moon peeked from behind the clouds to briefly reveal his face,

"Nice shoes, Brett."

I brought that shovel down with a loud grunt. Poor Brett had no time to react as the blade dug deep into his throat with as much ease as had the damp soil when Claire and I had dug our hole. Brett, as it turned out, was to be the first secret buried in there.

I stood quietly and watched the thick gush of blood pump from my would-be assailant's throat. Brett grasped at the wound with his good hand as if he actually had a chance of stemming the flow – his blood, rendered black in the silvery moonlight, simply spurted between his fingers as he died.

When Brett quit moving, I kicked him with my bare foot. No response.

Yup, he was definitely dead.

As my adrenaline rush wore off, I realized I'd forgotten all about Mark. He was still out there, quite likely lost in the darkness between the trees.

I made my way back to the main street, eschewing all attempts at stealth – I *wanted* Mark to hear me. I'd put an end to Brett's miserable, bullying life without as much as scratch on my body. I figured killing Mark with at least a little injury to myself would carry some dignity. Closer to the street, I heard a soft sound from the tree above me.

It sounded like sobbing.

"Mark?"

"I saw what you did to Brett," Mark's pitiful voice came from the dark – he didn't sound quite so tough without his buddy backing him up. "Please, I won't tell anyone. This has gone too far. *Please...*"

"Come on, Mark, at least lose like a man." There was bravado in my voice – I felt strong, all-powerful.

"It wasn't supposed to be like this," Mark sobbed.

"You made fun of my dead sister and were going to egg my house. What did you think was going to happen, Mark?"

It did occur to me that killing Brett had been an overreaction, but I could muster no regret. Situations like mine have a tendency of going astray; I'd simply been pushed too far.

"I-I-I didn't think you would fight b-b-back." Mark sobbed uncontrollably.

"Come down, Mark," I said. "Brett left me no choice. But you can surrender. Come on down, man. I'm not leaving, and you can't stay up there forever."

"Okay, but please don't hurt me."

"Let's talk."

Mark scrambled down from the tree and attempted to make a dash in the direction of the street. I grabbed his shoulder and stopped him.

"I heard you guys on the church basketball court. I was hiding behind the electric box with Claire."

"Who's Claire?"

I ignored him. "Why did you talk shit about my sister?"

"I got caught up in the moment," Mark sniffled. "My family thinks she deserved it."

"Why?"

"Because of what Lima said. I'm sorry, man."

"Was it Erin who planned all this? Because I wouldn't take the money?"

"Are you going to hurt her, too?"

"Don't worry about Erin, Mark. Just answer my question."

"No, you are going to hurt Erin, aren't you!" Mark squared up to me.

"Why so tough now, Mark?"

"She's my girlfriend!"

"So… it's Erin or your mom?" I knew precisely the right thing to say terrorize a weak mind.

"What?"

"I hurt Erin… or I hurt your mom."

"Listen, *nigger*," Mark snarled. "I was only going to mess up your house – but you fucking *killed* Brett, and I saw you! Who would be in more trouble?"

"You're right, Mark, but *you* made fun of my dead sister."

I swung the shovel across Mark's legs. The sharp edge sliced open his pants at the thigh, along with the soft flesh beneath – metal *clanked* sickeningly against bone, and Mark fell to the ground. His scream, when it came, tore through the silence of the night; I stopped it with the flat side of the shovel. As I pressed the cold metal against Mark's face, his screams persisted, but were muffled, and I heard a distinct *pop, pop* as his front teeth left their sockets.

"I'm gonna be nicer to you then I was to Brett," I said, moving the shovel from his face and down to his crotch. He winced as I pressed it down hard upon where I reckoned his dick was.

Then I let go.

"I can really hurt you, Mark." I stated the glaringly obvious. "But if you stand up and follow me, I won't. If you run or refuse, I'll cut your fucking dick off. Now, stand up."

Mark obliged the best he could with his sliced leg – his pants gaped open, drenched glistening wet with blood, and I'm sure I caught a glimpse of pink/red thigh bone through the raw flesh. I helped Mark walk back to the Hole of Secrets before pushing him in.

"I'm not going to torture you, Mark," I said with a weary tone; I was done with the blood and the violence – I just wanted to go home.

Mark peered up at me from the hole I'd dug with my dear, sweet Claire. His eyes were wide with terror in the silvery moonlight, his face smeared with dirt, tears, and snot

– he looked as wretched as he and his nasty little friends had made me feel for so very long.

"Goodbye, Mark."

The shovel connected hard and heavy with Mark's temple; the skin there split wide open as the sound of shattering skull rose high into the tree canopy in the darkness above us. Mark let out a loud, wheezing grunt and slumped face-first into the mushy mud at the bottom of the hole.

I reckoned the fucker was dead before he hit the dirt.

Satisfied with my handiwork – I just knew Claire and Sarah would be proud of me – I retrieved Brett's fat ass and dumped him into the hole alongside his partner-in-crime. It took me a while to roll Brett over, even though his corpse lay not twenty inches from its makeshift grave – that's what ya get for being so goddamned fat, Brett!

I rested awhile, then spent an hour or so – I kinda lost track – burying my tormentors until the sun began to peek over the horizon. Done, I patted the earth down flat and kicked leaves and twigs over the grave, and figured no one would ever know there was a hole with two dead schoolkids right there. Finally, I buried the shovel beneath a thin layer of leaf litter and moss – the murder weapon would rot there forever.

Back home, I threw the paint cans, screwdrivers, and eggs into the neighbors' trash cans – sharing them between three left out on the curbside for early morning collection. Then, I let myself into my house and made my way upstairs. My parents were still asleep, the house deathly quiet. I stripped off my muddy, blood-spattered clothes and climbed into the shower. I set the water as hot as I could bare it on my naked skin, and felt the loose dirt wash off my feet.

As the dirt washed away, along with any guilt at what I'd done, my mind drifted to thoughts of my beautiful Claire. I'd not given her a second thought once Brett and Mark were secreted beneath the woodland floor, nor had I gone back to see if she was still hiding behind my neighbor's bushes.

I didn't know it at the time, but it wasn't just me Brett, Mark, and Claire among the trees that night. Someone else, someone consumed entirely by the darkness, was also there.

End

Epilogue

January

Huntsville Texas

"Ishmael, I'm sure you are aware of the statute of limitations?"

"No, Doctor. So many years tied up in the legal system but no, never heard of that," Ishmael said with snarling sarcasm.

"Very well," replied Dr. Russell. The impact of what he'd just heard broke through his normally reserved demeanor. "Then, as you know, there is no statute of limitations for murder. So, there must be another explanation for you coming clean now."

Ishmael, his intelligence so obviously insulted, became visibly frustrated. "Did you think I was hoping you'd keep a secret?"

"My apologies. This is quite a lot for me to process."

"Stop trying to feign a natural reaction, Doctor," Ishmael snapped. "I know all of the things you've seen in your career."

"I feel we are digressing. Let's start again – from the top. One more time, Ishmael. Please," Dr. Russell said. He was desperate to not have to address Ishmael's retort because he was right: Dr. Lance Russell was emotionally numb to depravity at this point in his life.

"I know what I saw after I got home," Ishmael continued. "Believe me or not, I really didn't give a fuck. A minivan approached the woods right after I showered. Its lights were off and it was moving slowly. Through my house's side window, I saw the van park and two men got out and walked quickly into the woods. They had a dog with them. About fifteen minutes later, they came back – each one carried something large over their shoulders. It looked like rolled-up carpet. They put them in the back of the van and soon they were gone."

Dr. Russell took in a deep breath. "Well, if you did, indeed, murder those two young men in the woods as you claim, that would be a plausible explanation for why no bodies were discovered. We still can't say for sure someone took the bodies – or that anyone other than you was in those woods at all. Do you know who the men were, by any chance?"

"Yes." Ishmael's tone was reserved.

"Do you want to tell me?"

"Lima…"

"*Pastor* Lima?" The Doctor sounded most doubtful. "You believe Pastor Lima and an accomplice loaded two dead children's bodies into a van and drove them away?"

"I couldn't see their faces clearly, but I knew it was them."

"That leaves two questions unexplained," Dr. Russell offered.

"Don't fucking bother," Ishmael snarled. "I'm not a fool, you know. I've had nothing but time to think in this rathole, and I know what seems off. First of all, I don't know why Lima would be there right after I killed those two fuckers. He must have known what everyone was planning against me. It was easy for them to keep me out of it in school, but other kids probably told their parents, siblings… I don't know. It must have gotten back to Lima and he was watching me and Claire the whole time – far enough away for us not to spot him. Or maybe the van was there all along and it was too dark to see it. I don't know, but he must have seen us all go into the woods but only me coming out. I don't know his initial motive – you know, like why he was there in the first place. Either he was there to stop those fuckers from egging our house or he was there to make sure they weren't caught. He couldn't have possibly known at the time it would be their last day alive.

"After I did what I did, Lima's motive must have changed. As I said, I don't know what his initial motive was, but I know covering for me must have become his new motive. You know as well as I do what went down in Ashford over years after that – the formation of Lima's cult revolved around that shit. So, he definitely had motive."

"Interesting theory, but I don't –"

"It was actually good for me," Ishmael interrupted. "The way Lima spun the story of Brett and Mark disappearing meant no eyes were on me. That entire dumb town of single-celled organisms couldn't put any logic together as long as they had a guy to follow and worship. That's all they ever wanted. To be led."

Evidently enjoying a sense of newfound confidence, Ishmael had assumed the role of the one doing the questioning, although Dr. Russell was truly there just to talk and listen.

"Fine, so maybe I didn't kill anyone and I hallucinated the murders," Ishmael said. "Go ahead with that. I killed that bitch Mrs. Allen, though. So why wouldn't I keep going?"

Dr. Russell had always suspected hallucinations on Ishmael's part, though he had never come forward with his hypothesis. Ishmael's intuition was particularly good on that day, and the doctor reminded himself Ishmael was a highly regarded intellectual and Harvard graduate like himself.

"Ishmael, I never cast any doubt that you were responsible for Brett and Mark. But as for Mrs. Allen, she died of a heart attack. You know this," Dr. Russell said bluntly.

As expected, Ishmael's newfound confidence was short-lived. His nostrils flared and his eyes squinted as he prepared to interrogate Dr. Russell after hearing the man discredit his murder of the fat old teacher.

"The heart attack got to her before I did," Ishmael defended. "The tainted insulin shot would have killed her, and you know it. *I* did that to her, and no fucking heart attack will take that away from me. I killed her, just as I killed Brett and Mark. Let it be known. Let their ugly families know what happened to their little bitch baby boys, Doctor. Tell them I did it." Ishmael raised his voice and hit his fists on the table. The shackles didn't let him hit hard, but the tension in the room grew thick as fog.

Officer Mistry was on alert and on his way over, but Dr. Russell glanced toward him with raised hand of reassurance. Officer Mistry could take any action he felt necessary to avoid a physical altercation, but he trusted Dr. Russell's control of the situation.

"Okay, I'll see it your way," the doctor said to Ishmael.

"Sounds like you're patronizing me, Doctor," Ishmael snapped back. How he wished he could escape the shackles securing him to the metal table bolted to the concrete floor; it limited his expression. "Let me ask you something. Supposing you *don't* believe me…"

"I never said I don't believe you, Ishmael."

Unperturbed, Ishmael continued, "*Suppose* you don't believe me. Then what do you make of Brett and Mark's disappearance?"

"This is just a hypothetical, Ishmael. Assuming I don't believe you, I would call attention to the fact that Brett and Mark were a disturbance to you. They were a source of great pain and abuse. Their disappearance, regardless of the circumstances behind it, was a great weight off of you. Sadly, it wasn't enough, because their disappearance brought you no salvation. Therefore, perhaps you dreamed the whole encounter of taking their lives, when in reality they disappeared for another reason."

"Now that's good psychology, Doctor!" Ishmael scoffed sarcastically.

Desperate to avoid escalation, Dr. Russell dialed it back. It felt cruel to antagonize – albeit inadvertently –a restrained man. "I never deduced that's what happened. But... it is my job to consider other explanations and rule them out."

"What about the most obvious thing you are ignoring?"

"Which is?" replied Dr. Russell.

"Why am I incarcerated in the first place?" Ishmael sat back in his chair nonchalantly, knowing he caught the doctor in a corner.

"I know why you are here, but the matter at hand is..."

"Remember what I did to the acquitted child predator in Fort Worth?"

"Ishmael, we don't need to relive and glamorize prior –" he responded before being interrupted.

"Let's not forget the breakfast restaurant owner in Houston in that strip center. Can't ever forget what I saw him doing in the car late at night," said Ishmael as he startled to chuckle. Reliving that night broke down his defensive wall and he started exhibiting his true nature in front of the doctor. "Took forever to find out where he worked."

"Ishmael, please," pleaded the Dr. Russell.

"Unfortunately, I couldn't find his car that night after I *bumped* him. Maybe he got a ride that day. I do feel bad for that sweet couple behind the strip center coming out of the Boba Tea place. I really do, being at the wrong place at the wrong time. That red Benz was a sweet ride. But I forgot never to underestimate the resolve of a guy with a gorgeous girl. Fucker got my face and broke my nose but I got his teeth and I cut his shins. I do feel bad though. They really didn't deserve it. Wish I got the car."

Patience running out, Dr. Russell raised his voice. "I wasn't aware of the strip center incident. I am thinking nobody knows about this except you three, however..." Dr. Russell continued before being interrupted.

"For real though, the gorgeous lady actually became famous after she was found in the woods dead but her baby was alive. Remember that story?"

"I am familiar with the story of the dentist in Houston, but are you telling me you had an altercation with this couple previously? I am not doubting you, and we can get back to this. But as of right now, I am fully aware of what actually landed you in prison. But the difference is you were an adult in Fort Worth and in Houston. But in Ashford Ohio, a child can have such resolve?"

"Then rule this out, Doctor." Ishmael looked Dr. Russell squarely in the face. "I know all you see me as is a *killer nigger*, but I do have my integrity. I *said* it happened and it did!" Then, in an instant, his voice relaxed as the high of reliving his prior crimes started to ease. "I see it in your eyes. You believe me, Doctor. Please stop playing psychology with me and talk to me like a fucking man. You are doubting me for a reason and you won't say what that reason is." Ishmael relaxed his shoulders and the expression on his face.

Ishmael's intuition was correct: Dr. Russell did indeed believe him, and he was right to do so. Ishmael did murder Brett and Mark, just as he had attempted to murder Mrs. Allen. Dr. Russell was also correct in that his job was to rule out alternatives. Ishmael was beginning to understand the motive for questioning him, and the doctor's sympathy helped him relax.

"And that's my fault. I'm all cool, Doctor. Sorry for reacting like that," Ishmael reassured. "Man to man, I know you know I did it. I know you believe it. So, what's the deal?"

"What made you look out of the window after you showered?" Dr. Russell asked with no hesitation.

"I heard Claire's voice."

"*Claire*? She was inside your house?"

"No, not like that." Ishmael paused a moment to gather his thoughts. "Well... I don't mean I *heard* her literally. I kind of *felt* her presence – like in my heart. She was my girlfriend after all. After I showered, I heard her voice in my mind and knew she was still outside. I looked out of the window towards the street and saw her. I wanted to go down to her, but she shook her head to tell me no. She pointed towards the minivan heading toward her in the middle of the street. She *wanted* me to see it. That's how I was able to watch everything that happened."

"Claire was in the street? And the minivan didn't stop?"

"I guess they just didn't see her. They kept going and drove right towards her…"

"I can imagine that's the last thing Sarah saw before she passed."

"Dr. Russell?" Ishmael's expression was as if he'd been stabbed in the heart. The cruel statement knocked him off his mental balance and shifted control of the conversation back to Dr. Russell.

"Man to man, Ishmael."

"Yeah, I suppose. But that didn't happen to Claire. When the minivan got to her, it just passed right through her."

"And how do you think that was possible?"

Ishmael sat in silence.

The realization Dr. Russell brought to the table wasn't anything new. Ishmael knew. He'd *always* known. He just didn't want to come to terms with it, so he'd kept it buried inside so deep that nothing within him could ever bring it out; so deep within him he didn't even realize it when he was telling Dr. Russell the stories of his troubled childhood. But there, in front of the doctor, Ishmael had been forced, for the first time, to face *reality*. He couldn't bring himself to say it: It would be like losing Sarah all over again.

"Ishmael…" Dr. Russell prompted.

His plea fell on deaf ears. Ishmael remained silent, but both men knew what deep realization had just come to the surface.

Ishmael glanced toward Officer Mistry and, minutes later, he was gone without as much as a goodbye.

***

Back in his cell, Ishmael was disgusted Dr. Russell would made such an insinuation. He was pretty much calling him a crazy person. Ishmael knew himself to be a dangerous criminal, but he was *not* crazy. His hands balled into fists and he prepared to punch the wall as his teeth trembled in explosive anger, when suddenly his rage was soothed. The soft, sweet smell of strawberry shampoo permeated the dusty concrete walls. A soft gentle touch ran up and down his left arm, relaxing his muscles to the point a feather could have felt as heavy as a brick.

He looked behind him, and in his cell stood a beautiful woman in her mid-thirties. Her blonde hair was down and covered her neck. She wore a pink camisole, cropped but only slightly. Remnants of scars were on her belly and sides, but long-healed now. She wore a black skirt that ended just above her knees.

Ishmael gasped, struggling to breathe.

The woman put her arms around Ishmael and pushed her mouth against his, reviving him with her warm breath.

"Didn't I say I would never leave you, Ishmael?" she asked.

With barely a breath, Ishmael's voice was barely a whimper.

"Claire," he said.

End of Book One

About the Author

Isaac Hans resides in Texas. He specializes in psychological thriller and horror novels. His trademark is each novel, while written in the horror style, is written to bring awareness to societal plagues and injustices in an effort to bring a different perspective on how these issues are prevalent, their negative impact, and how they need to be eradicated as a society.

He has one novel currently published, Neha's Mother, a horror-filled and suspenseful tale about unconditional love, and is currently available on Amazon.com.

When not writing, Hans is an avid reader, with his favorite authors being Stephen King, William Peter Blatty, Shirley Jackson, and Ira Levin. His favorite novels are Rosemary's Baby and The Exorcist.

His favorite films are Aniara, The Conjuring, Event Horizon. But it's not all horror, as Issac loves to watch Toy Story and Cocomelon with this daughter.

Hans is currently working the sequel to Neha's Mother, currently called The Bride is too Dark, with an anticipated release date in late 2022.

http://isaachansauthor.com/

Also by Isaac Hans

Andrei Ivanov, a lonely, single father is awoken suddenly one night by his three-year-old daughter, Natalia, sleepwalking during a violent thunderstorm.

Little does Andrei know, but this disturbing incident is only the beginning of a series of terrifying events in which his life will begin to unravel at a breathtaking pace.

At the hands of a malevolent, otherworldly entity, which lays claim to Natalia, Andrei experiences horrifying hallucinations, family tragedy, murder, and the suspicious death of the prominent physician who was to treat his little girl for her erratic behavior.

As he spirals into an unstoppable nightmare, Andrei begins to question his sanity as he learns the true nature of his adversary and realizes he faces an unearthly battle to save his daughter's eternal soul.